Lucky Foot Stable Series

"Dawson's experience as an educator and director of an Equine Institute serve her well in these novels."
 —Troy Michelle Reinhardt
 ForeWord Magazine

"Anyone who enjoys a great tale of horses and youth will find this a fascinating read. This most entertaining story moves swiftly in a non-preaching way while dealing with some very real issues...peer pressure, decision making, responsibility, self-esteem, and learning to care about others."
 —Ellie Mencer
 Lockhouse to Lighthouse Magazine

"The author's love of horses shines through as she captures the quintessential passion held by many young girls for their animal."
 —Paula F. Kelly
 The News Journal

"Combines adventure with valuable lessons on life and friendship. Dawson has created believable characters with a love of horses."
 —*The Equiery*

"Creates an entertaining way to teach young riders the value of horses."
 —Stephanie Stephens
 Stable Management Magazine

Mary and Jody in the Movies

JoAnn S. Dawson

Illustrated by Michelle Keenan

SOURCEBOOKS Jabberwocky
AN IMPRINT OF SOURCEBOOKS

Sourcebooks and the colophon are registered trademarks of Sourcebooks, Inc.

Published by Sourcebooks Jabberwocky, an imprint of Sourcebooks, Inc.
P.O. Box 4410, Naperville, Illinois 60567-4410
(630) 961-3900
Fax: (630) 961-2168
www.sourcebooks.com

Library of Congress Cataloging-in-Publication Data

Dawson, JoAnn.
   Mary and Jody in the movies / Joann S. Dawson; illustrated by Michelle Keenan.
       p. cm. — (Lucky Foot Stable; bk. 4)
   Summary: Everyone is excited when the McMurray dairy farm is chosen to be the
setting of a movie, especially best friends Mary and Jody who see it as an opportu-
nity to show off their ponies Lady and Gypsy.
   ISBN-13: 978-1-4022-0999-4 (alk. paper)
   ISBN-10: 1-4022-0999-1 (alk. paper)
   [1. Motion pictures—Production and direction—Fiction. 2. Ponies—Fiction. 3.
Horsemanship—Fiction. 4. Farm life—Fiction.] I. Keenan, Michelle, ill. II. Title.
   PZ7.D32735Mar 2008
   [Fic]—dc22
                                    2008008494

                 Printed and bound in the United States of America.
                     VP 10 9 8 7 6 5 4 3 2 1

To Aunt Edie and Aunt Kathryn

Lucky Foot Stable

Contents

★ 1 ★

Invasion of the Movie People

J ODY HAD JUST put the finishing touches on Star's mane, combing it just as Willie had shown her, while Mary vigorously swept the dirt floor of Lucky Foot Stable of wayward wisps of straw when they first heard the rumble. Star lifted his head, pricked his ears, and strained against the cross-ties to get a better look out the back doors of the little white stable. Finnegan, the cow-herding dog, suddenly awoke from a deep slumber and growled low in his throat as the rumble grew louder.

"What in the..." Mary began, exchanging worried

looks with Jody. Then, in unison, Mary threw down her broom and Jody stuck the comb in the crest of Star's mane where it dangled dangerously. Racing down the aisle, they reached the open doors of the stable at the exact same instant and stared open-mouthed at the spectacle before them.

Proceeding down the long gravel lane of the McMurray dairy farm were not one, not two, but four large, boxy white trucks, veering this way and that to avoid the deep potholes randomly pitting the driveway. Finnegan ran circles around the two girls and barked madly, all the while wagging his tail in anticipation of visitors as the trucks continued toward the McMurray's stone farmhouse, raising clouds of dust as they went.

"What in the..." Jody echoed. The girls linked arms and squinted to read the black words painted on the side of the first truck in line as it turned slightly at the bend in the lane.

"Hanley's...what does it say?" Mary asked impatiently. "I can't see the rest of it. The dust is too thick."

"It says...it says...Hanley's Film...Hanley's Film and Cinema Equipment. I think that's what it says," Jody said doubtfully.

★ 2 ★

"Film and cinema equipment!" Mary shrieked. "Of course that's what is says! Jody, it's the movie people! They're here! They're going to start the movie! They need someone to greet them! Let's go!"

With that, Mary took off at a gallop across the grass, and Jody started after her but suddenly stopped in her tracks.

"Mare, wait!" Jody yelled. "I left Star on crossties! I've got to put him back in his stall! Wait for me."

It took all of Mary's effort to stand still and watch as the trucks reached the farmhouse without her, but stand she did, jiggling impatiently as she waited for Jody to emerge from the stable. She had just started to bite her fingernails when Jody finally joined her, followed by the ecstatic Finnegan, who yipped excitedly in anticipation of a new adventure.

"Mary, maybe Mr. McMurray doesn't want us to greet the movie people," Jody reasoned, linking her arm in Mary's to slow her progress toward the trucks, now parked in a row in front of the farmhouse. "Maybe he wants us to stay away until he invites us to meet them. And don't forget what Willie said."

"I know, I know, Willie said wait to speak until spoken to. But, Jody, what if Mr. McMurray isn't home right now? And I know Willie is down in the barn with the cows. It's milking time, and he won't be done for another hour at least, even with Mr. Mooney helping him."

Willie had rarely missed a milking in the thirty years he had worked on the McMurray dairy farm, even after Mr. McMurray hired a younger man to help out around the barn. Mr. Roy Mooney had arrived the year before with his teenaged son, Jimmy, his daughter Annie, and a toddler named Heath. After Mr. Mooney's wife died, he had been forced to sell his own farm, and Mr. McMurray had offered him the job helping Willie. Jimmy helped his father with the farm work while Annie watched Heath in the old house trailer where the family lived.

"But, you know, Jody," Mary continued, hardly stopping to take a breath, "Willie is just going to have to get used to the fact that he can't milk cows every day, now that he's the wrangler on the movie. He's going to have to work with the horses and the actors. Including us."

"Us?" Jody giggled. "Mare, we're not exactly actors."

"Well, remember what Mr. Crowley said. They need us to be in the riding lesson scenes. And Willie will probably be there telling us what to do, since he's the head wrangler, and…"

Before Mary could finish her sentence, Jody grabbed her by the arm and stopped them both in their tracks. "Finnegan, stay," she commanded the excited dog, who sat obediently but couldn't help whining and wagging his tail so that his whole body wagged along. The girls had just about reached the farmhouse, where a crew of men was busy unloading the first of the four trucks. Mary and Jody watched in awe as two of the men grabbed the bottom of the back door of the third truck and shoved upward. The door buckled like an accordion and disappeared into the top section of the truck, revealing the equipment inside.

"Just like a garage door," Jody whispered. "That is so cool!"

The double red doors of the stone farmhouse suddenly burst open, and Mr. McMurray appeared, strode down the steps, and beckoned grandly to the crew of men.

"Come on in, then, we've cleared a space for you!" Mr. McMurray directed in his booming Irish brogue. "Right here, and over there…now what can I help you with?"

"Well, Jode, I guess Mr. McMurray *is* here," Mary said, disappointed that they weren't needed as greeters after all.

"And boy, he sounds happy, too!" Jody said, smiling as she watched the kindly farmer bustling around the trucks of film equipment.

"Of course he's happy!" Mary agreed. "This movie is going to save the farm, after all."

It was only a few months before when Mr. McMurray had fallen ill and undergone an operation on his heart. The medical bills that followed had forced him to consider selling the farm, until the miraculous day when Mr. Ted Crowley, movie location scout, had arrived, looking for a dairy just like Mr. McMurray's to use in a motion picture.

"And it's going to save Star and Willie and us, too, in a way," Jody murmured.

The girls watched in silence then as the men continued unloading blue and yellow metal boxes of all shapes and sizes, long black poles, ladders, fat green and black extension cords, and all manner of things Mary and Jody had never seen before. Just as the last box came off the truck and disappeared into the McMurray farmhouse, Finnegan suddenly spun around to face the gravel lane and once again set up a howl. When Mary and Jody turned to see what the commotion was about, their mouths flew open for the second time that day.

Roaring up the gravel lane, one after the other, came a whole caravan of trucks, the first in line pulling a long flatbed trailer. And sitting atop the trailer was a huge yellow bulldozer. Following that, a flatbed truck with piles of wood posts and boards secured to the truck with thick metal straps. Then a long, white, enclosed truck with the words *A&C Tent Rentals* emblazoned on the side. Finally, a shorter black truck and trailer bearing a drawing of a smiling cat next to the words *ThomCats Catering, Movie Division.*

Mary and Jody watched openmouthed in amazement as the caravan made its way to an open field between the farmhouse and the big, white dairy barn. This was where Mr. McMurray usually parked his farm equipment, but Mr. Mooney had moved everything the week before to make room for the movie crews.

"Shut yer mouths, yer catchin' flies," a familiar voice suddenly commanded from behind the two girls.

"Willie!" Mary shouted, spinning to face the cowhand. "Oh my gosh! Did you see all those trucks?

And all the men? Did you see all the stuff they unloaded?"

"Do they need all that stuff just to make a movie?" Jody chimed in.

"All that stuff? Why, they ain't even half finished yet. That's just part of it. And there'll be a lot more crew members here before it's all over."

"But, Willie, what about the bulldozer? And the boards and the posts? Are they building a whole new pasture field?" Mary asked.

"No, not a pasture field," Willie replied mysteriously.

"Well, what then? They must be getting ready to dig up the ground for some reason and build a fence," Mary reasoned.

"Well, what else can you think of that needs a clear space, and a lot of dirt, and maybe some sand, and has to be closed in with a fence?" Willie replied with a smile.

The girls looked at each other quizzically for a moment. Then the light of understanding dawned on Mary's face, and she grabbed Jody's arm and began wordlessly jumping up and down.

"What, Mare? What is it?" Jody giggled as Finnegan yipped and jumped right along with Mary.

Jody giggled as Finnegan yipped
and jumped right along with Mary.

"Jode! What do you think? It's a ring! A ring for us to ride in! Just like at the horse shows!"

Jody's eyes flew open wide and she turned again to Willie. "Willie, is it true? Are they really building a real ring? Will we be allowed to ride in it?"

"Well, I guess they are, and sure, you'll be riding in it—that is, if you behave yourselves and don't act simple. They want people in the movie that they can count on to act right and listen to what they say," Willie explained, looking pointedly at Mary.

"Willie, you know I can be quiet and listen when I have to," Mary pouted. "Like just now, I did what you said. I didn't speak to the movie people. I'm waiting for them to speak to me."

Upon hearing this speech, Jody crossed her arms and shot Mary an agitated look, which Mary promptly ignored.

"Hmmm," Willie smiled, comprehending the reason for Jody's dismay. "Well, just remember what I said and don't make nuisances of yourselves."

"We promise, Willie," Jody said confidently. "I'll make sure of it."

2

Willie Explains It All

BY THE END of the day, enough trucks and trailers had rumbled up the McMurray farm lane to fill almost the entire field where the farm equipment had once been. Mary and Jody watched the unloading process from afar, taking heed of Willie's orders not to make a nuisance of themselves. But Mary was about to burst, wanting to get closer—especially to see what was contained in the trucks that were yet to be opened.

"Jody, maybe Mrs. McMurray needs help gathering the eggs this afternoon," Mary said innocently, just as the last truck was parked securely in the field. "We could go up to the house and ask her."

"Mare, you know Mrs. McMurray doesn't need help with the eggs," Jody said sternly. "You just want to go up to the house to see what's going on."

"Well, don't you?" Mary fairly shouted. "We could just go up and look around a little bit!"

"I have a better idea," Jody replied sensibly. "Why don't we go bring Lady and Gypsy in from the pasture and groom them. Star's still in the stable all by himself, so I'm sure he'd like the company. And besides, it'll keep our minds off of the movie for a while!"

"Oh, all right," Mary agreed reluctantly. "I guess we have been neglecting them for the past few days, we've been so busy working with Star."

Star of Wonder, the ornery colt, was just going on nineteen months old that July, and with Willie's help, Mary and Jody had finally trained him well enough to begin putting a little bit of weight on his back. He was already accustomed to the saddle and bridle, and the girls had been placing burlap sacks filled with hay across his back to get him used to the feel of it, in anticipation of riding.

"Gypsy! Ladabucks! We're coming to get you!" Mary called in a singsong voice as the girls trotted across the pasture toward the weeping willow tree that shaded the two ponies from the hot July sun. The black and white dairy cows in the field raised their heads curiously, chewing their cuds as the girls went by. Then, they lowered them again and continued grazing.

"Hey, Jode! I just got a great idea!" Mary said enthusiastically, clipping the lead rope onto Gypsy's halter. "Why don't we ride the ponies up to the house so the movie people can see how beautiful and well-behaved they are for riding in the movie?"

"Mary," Jody groaned impatiently, "first of all, I don't think the men unloading the trucks are the ones who make the decision about which horses to use in the movie. And second of all, I promised Willie I would keep you under control."

"Oh, you're such a party pooper!" Mary yelped, her feelings hurt. "And besides, you don't have to keep me under control. I can do that just fine by myself, thank you."

Jody felt sorry for what she had said, but she led Lady toward the gate without a word, Mary following with Gypsy. The girls entered Lucky Foot Stable in silence and cross-tied the two ponies in the aisle, gathering up their brushes from their tack boxes.

The only sounds to be heard in the little white barn were the gentle snores of Finnegan asleep on a pile of straw in the corner and an occasional cluck-cluck from Colonel Sanders, the old barn rooster, glaring down at the girls from his perch on the top board of Lady's stall.

Mary and Jody were so intent on brushing the ponies and not talking to each other that they didn't hear Willie enter the stable.

"Why's it so quiet in here?" Willie asked suddenly. "You might think somebody died or somethin'."

The girls continued grooming without a word. Willie hobbled over to Star's stall and began scratching him behind the ears.

"Well, does anybody want to hear some good news?" Willie addressed the air. Mary and Jody still didn't speak but slowed their furious brushing and pricked up their ears.

"Hmph, well, I guess not. I'll just have to keep it to myself," he said and turned to walk out the back doors of the stable.

"Willie, I want to hear the good news!" Jody called, unable to keep quiet a moment longer.

"Me, too!" Mary chimed in, dropping her brushes and joining Jody in the back of the stable, proud of herself for not being the first to break the silence.

Willie turned to face the expectant girls, trying his best to hide the smile that had crept across his face. "I talked to the film producers today," he began, tugging on his earlobe as he always did when he had news to share. "Or I guess maybe I should say, they talked to me."

"What about, Willie?" the girls asked in unison, then burst into giggles, forgetting they were supposed to be mad at each other.

"Now, do either one of you remember the problem we had that was gonna be solved by the movie comin' here? Other than the farm being saved, that is," Willie asked a bit sarcastically.

"Of course we remember, Willie!" Mary said indignantly. "We have to pay the two thousand dollar breeding fee to the nasty man who thinks he owns half of Star, or he's going to take him away from us! How could we forget that?"

"Now, how many times do I have to tell ya, he's not a nasty man. He just has to keep track of all the foals that his champion stallion sires, and he has a legal right to Star. We're lucky he's takin' the money, and not the colt." Willie answered.

Mary and Jody stood breathless for a moment, afraid to ask the next question. It was finally Jody who found her voice.

"Willie, what do you mean? Is he going to accept the money? Do we have the money to give him?" she whispered, grasping Mary's hand.

"Well, that's what I come to tell you. The producers agreed to give me an advance on my wrangler salary, and I'm gettin' it by the end of the week. So when I get it, I can turn it over to the man, and it'll be done and over with."

The girls looked at each other wordlessly, tears springing to their eyes. Then, as one, they rushed to Willie and threw their arms around him in a bear hug.

"Thank you ever so, Willie," Mary mumbled, tears flowing down her cheeks. Jody couldn't speak but instead squeezed Willie as hard as she could.

"Now, now, quit yer foolishness, yer chokin' me to death," Willie said, trying to sound grumpy as he disentangled himself from the two grateful girls. "It'll be supper time before you know it, and I got to go chop some silage for the cows."

"But, Willie, before you go, when can we talk to the movie people?" Mary blurted, forgetting she was supposed to be patient. The instant the sentence flew out, she clapped her hand over her mouth and flushed beet red.

Willie smiled in spite of himself and shook his head. "If you go ahead and get these ponies turned out and get on home for a decent night's sleep, I'll introduce you to some of them tomorrow. I'm goin' to be seein' at least one old friend, I'm told. And they're goin' to start buildin' the ring tomorrow, too."

"Already? They're going to build the ring right now?" Jody asked incredulously.

Willie scratched his head and hobbled over to sit on a bale of hay in front of Star's stall. "Sit there on the tack trunk, and let me explain some things to you two before you go off half crazy."

Mary and Jody obediently sat on Mary's tack trunk and waited breathlessly for Willie's explanation.

"First of all, things get done real quick on a movie set, as far as buildin' and constructin' sets and things. You gotta understand, they only have two to three months to film the movie, so that's one reason they have so many people—to get things done in a hurry. Now, since you two might be asked to be in a couple of the ridin' scenes, there's some things you have to know."

"Sit there on the tack trunk, and let me explain some things to you two before you go off half crazy."

Mary and Jody grinned and clapped their hands joyously at the thought of actually being in a real movie.

"Now, before you get all excited, it's not as glamorous as everybody thinks it is," Willie went on sternly. "It's work. A lot of hard work. And it's monotonous. Sometimes it takes a whole day to film one little part that will end up bein' about a minute in the movie. Or that part could get cut out altogether. Sometimes you have to do your scene over and over until the director thinks it's just right. So you can't get impatient, or tired and grumpy, or mouthy with the people in charge." In spite of himself, Willie addressed this last part to Mary, who quickly took offense.

"Willie," she said solemnly, "I know you think I can't keep quiet sometimes, but I can. I promise I won't get tired and grumpy and mouthy. And I will listen to whatever the director tells me."

Willie just nodded and then turned to Jody. "But you also don't want to be too shy. If you have somethin' to say, or some kind of problem on the set, or if you see somethin' dangerous goin' on, don't be afraid to tell somebody."

Then it was Jody's turn to nod silently, taking in everything Willie was saying.

"Willie, what is the movie about, anyway?" Mary asked suddenly. "We don't even know anything about the story."

"Well, as far as I can tell, it's about a city boy who meets a country girl in college and starts to come out to help her daddy on the farm, mostly to impress her. He ends up fallin' for her and learnin' some lessons from the farm, but he's got some competition from another country boy. Through some kind of misunderstandin', the city boy and the country girl break up, even though he still loves her, and he gets a job workin' for a big-time land developer."

"Uh-oh," Mary said.

"Uh-oh is right, because then he finds out that the developer is going to encourage his buddies at the bank to foreclose on the farm because it's so far in debt. That way, the developer can buy the land and build houses on it. So the city boy has to decide if he wants to help save the farm and try to get the girl back, or keep his big-time job with the developer. Of course, his parents want him to keep the job, and so on."

"So where do the horses come in?" Jody asked.

"Well, one of the things the country girl does is teach a few riding lessons on the farm to try to help out with the debt. And she also rides her own horse and helps to herd the heifers and round up the cows."

"Wow. Sounds like a good story," Mary said.

"We'll see," Willie said cautiously. "Now, like I said, get these ponies turned out to pasture and get Star taken care of, and get on home. Mary, don't forget to tell your mama, and Jody, tell your daddy the good news about Star, so they can quit frettin' about it. And be here bright and early tomorrow on your best behavior, so I won't be embarrassed to show you to the movie people."

Annie Appears

THE NEXT MORNING, by pre-arrangement, Mary and Jody were up at the crack of dawn, ready to hop on their bikes and ride to Lucky Foot Stable from their homes at opposite ends of the road. Mary tried to be very quiet and not wake her mother, who worked as an accountant and didn't have to be at work until later in the morning. But before she had the chance to sneak out the door, Mrs. Morrow appeared in the kitchen and handed her a paper bag.

"Mary, give this to Willie," she said, yawning. "I packed him a nice lunch and put some of my chocolate cake in there, which I know he likes. And you girls be sure and tell him how much it means to you that he is giving up some of his pay to save Star-baby."

Mary's mother always added "baby" to the end of Star's name, even though he was practically grown up now. And even though Star really belonged to Jody, because he was Lady's colt, Mrs. Morrow knew how much he meant to Mary as well.

"Mom, we already told him. He knows how grateful we are, and he gets kind of embarrassed when we make a fuss over him. But I'll give him the lunch and the cake!"

Mrs. Morrow stood at the kitchen door and watched as Mary climbed onto her bike and placed the paper bag gently in the wire basket on the front. "Be careful!" she called, waving as Mary pedaled down the driveway.

Mary and Jody arrived at the farm lane on their bikes at the exact same instant, and from there it was a race to the "finish line," which was really the back doors of Lucky Foot Stable.

"Last one there is a rotten egg!" Mary yelled, pedaling furiously just a hair in front of Jody. But by the time they reached their destination, Mary was winded, and Jody braked to a halt just outside the doors, beating Mary by about a foot.

"Guess that means I'm a rotten egg," Mary giggled.

"You do smell kind of funny," Jody teased, flinging open the back doors and striding down the aisle of Lucky Foot with Mary close behind. They reached the Dutch doors at the front of the stable and leaned over to greet Star, who nickered to them from the other side of the paddock and then stretched his legs like a dog before ambling over for his morning treat.

"I wonder if the movie people are even here yet," Jody wondered as Star munched contentedly on the carrot she offered him.

"They probably are. Willie said they get here really early, because it takes a long time to set everything up before they start filming."

"Let's go look," Jody said. "It can't hurt just to look, can it? Then, when Willie gets done milking, he can introduce us to everybody."

Mary didn't say a word as she followed Jody out of the stable. She wasn't about to remind her that Willie had said to wait for him before they went up to see the movie set.

Before the girls had gone even halfway up the lane, they could see that things on the farm had definitely changed since the day before. To the left of the chicken house where Mrs. McMurray collected the eggs each day from her Rhode Island Red hens stood a huge white tent, its peaks pointing to the sky. More long white trailers had arrived, each with four or five doors on one side and metal steps with railings leading up to the doors.

Mary and Jody could see that on each door hung a small white sign, but from their position in the lane, they couldn't make out what was written on the signs. What they could see was that painted on the side of one of the trailers were the words *Honey Wagon* next to a drawing of a smiling honeybee.

"Honey wagon? I wonder what that means," Mary asked herself. Then she sniffed the air as they got closer to the farmhouse.

"Something smells really good," she exclaimed, linking arms with Jody. "Do you think Mrs. McMurray is cooking breakfast for everybody?"

"No, Mare, I don't think Mrs. McMurray is cooking," Jody replied, pointing to the left of the farmhouse.

There, just steps from where Mrs. McMurray's clothesline hung in the yard, stood the black trailer they had seen the day before, the one with the grinning cat painted on its side. A long, hinged door on the side of the trailer had been dropped open to reveal an entire kitchen inside. Three men were bustling around inside the trailer with spatulas in their hands, and fragrant smoke and steam rose from the cooktops. On the sidewalk outside the trailer stood four long tables covered with white linen tablecloths. Atop the tables sat lidded metal pans with flames underneath, piles of plates and napkins, baskets of silverware, coffee pots, several trays of doughnuts and bagels, cups and bowls, and best of all, a glass container full of all sorts of candy. But the most amazing part of the spectacle was the number of people, men and women, some milling around the tables, some standing in line in front of the black trailer shouting their breakfast orders, and some speaking on walkie-talkies.

"Gosh, Mare," Jody breathed in awe, "do you think all these people are here just to make a movie?"

"Remember what Willie said yesterday, Jody. It takes a lot of people to get everything set up. Maybe they're all just here to get the set ready, and then they'll go away."

Just then, the deafening roar of a revving engine made the girls jump. When they swung around to look behind them for the source of the noise, yet another astonishing sight met their eyes. Creeping across the lane, its giant tracks propelling it slowly forward toward Mr. McMurray's wheat field, was the yellow bulldozer they had seen arriving the day before. Plumes of black smoke puffed from its stack as it chugged along.

"They must be getting ready to build the ring already, just like Willie said," Mary exclaimed. "Let's go see where they're going to put it!"

Mary and Jody followed the bulldozer around to the rear of the farmhouse and all the way to the edge of the wheat field, where now only stubbles remained after the previous week's wheat harvest. Already unloaded and stacked to the side of the field were the posts and boards the girls had seen strapped to the flatbed trailer the day before.

"Wow, people must have been working all last night to get all of this done already," Jody observed.

"They were," said an unexpected voice from behind the two girls. Mary and Jody turned to find Annie Mooney standing directly behind them.

Annie was Mr. Mooney's red-haired, bespectacled daughter. She spent most of her time in the house trailer on the farm, looking after two-year-old Heath while Jimmy and her father worked on the farm. But she occasionally came out to visit Mary and Jody and

*Mary and Jody turned to find Annie Mooney
standing directly behind them.*

the ponies, and she almost always seemed to appear out of nowhere.

"Annie! We didn't see you there!" Mary said. "What do you mean? Were you out here last night?"

"For a while," Annie replied.

Mary and Jody waited expectantly for Annie to continue, but one thing they knew about her was that getting her to speak was like "pulling hen's teeth," as Willie would say. So Jody took over the questioning, knowing that Annie's natural tendency to keep things to herself would drive Mary crazy.

"So, Annie, what were they doing out here last night?" Jody asked sweetly.

"Well, they unloaded the fence, and they set up the tent," she said. "Oh, and the food trailer."

"Uh-huh," Jody said, "so they must have been working pretty late, huh?"

"Yep," Annie nodded.

"Annie, did you talk to any of them?" Mary asked, suddenly fearful that Annie had gotten the upper hand.

"Nope."

"OK, then," Mary said, after waiting for Annie to continue, to no avail. "Well, Annie, we have to go find Willie now."

"OK, see ya," Annie replied. Then she turned and was gone.

Mary and Jody watched for another minute as the bulldozer dug its teeth into the stubble of the wheat field, exposing the dark, rich soil underneath. Then they turned to go back to the farmhouse to find Willie and meet the "movie people."

The Farm
Transformed

MARY AND JODY saw Finnegan before they saw Willie. The friendly dog was in his glory, mingling with the movie people, wagging his tail, offering his paw, and licking one face after another as they leaned down to pet him and give him treats from the food table.

"Look at Finney," Mary laughed. "He's trying out for a part in the movie."

"Hey, there's Willie, too," Mary said, pointing at a group of men talking on the stoop of the farmhouse. "Do you think it's OK to go over there now, Mare?"

"Of course it is, Jody. Willie said he would introduce us, and it's about time, too," Mary said confidently. "After all, we *are* going to be in the movie and everything."

Jody sighed, hoping Mary wasn't already getting "too big for her britches," as Willie would say. Before she could reply, Mary was striding across the grass toward the group of men, and Jody had no choice but to follow.

"Hi, Willie!" Mary called, waving as she approached the group. "We're here!"

The men in the group looked up as one and grinned at the sight of the two girls, while Willie began pulling on his earlobe and scratching the side of his head. Then Mary spotted another familiar face in the crowd.

"Mr. Crowley!" she shouted. "It's me, Mary! Remember when we met on the day you came out to look at the farm?"

"Well, of course I remember you, Mary," Mr. Crowley said, shaking Mary's hand. "It's good to see you again. And I believe this is your friend..."

"Jody. That's Jody. We keep our ponies—Star, Lady, and Gypsy—here on the farm. They're really good ponies, and they're all ready to be in the movie. If you need them, that is. And I remember you said you might need some girls to ride in the movie, too, and we would really like to help you out with that, too, and…"

"Mary, Mary," Willie interrupted. "Slow down. Mr. Crowley was in the middle of a conversation here."

"Oh, I'm sorry, sir," Mary said, clapping her hand over her mouth.

"That's quite all right, Mary. We were just going over some of the details of the film. And, yes, I believe we do need some girls to ride in a couple of scenes, and we might need your ponies, too. So thank you for offering your assistance."

Mary grinned, and Jody could see it was all she could do to refrain from clapping and jumping up and down.

Willie shook his head and glanced apologetically at the other men in the group, who were still smiling at Mary and Jody.

"Well, I told these girls I would introduce them, since they'll be buggin' me to death otherwise," Willie said. "So, Mary and Jody, this is Mr. Gordon. He's the director of the picture."

"Pleased to meet you," said Mr. Gordon, nodding cordially.

"And this is Mr. Manzella, the main cameraman."

Mr. Manzella winked and gave the girls a "thumbs up."

"And this is Twister. He's goin' to be helpin' me with the wrangler work. We worked together years ago."

"Howdy, girls, glad to know ya," Twister said in a deep gravelly voice. He tipped his cowboy hat to the girls, and when he smiled, Mary and Jody were astonished to see that his two front teeth were missing completely. He was tall and thin, with straggly shoulder-length gray hair and a handlebar mustache. Mary and Jody had never seen anyone who looked quite like Twister.

"Hi, Twister," Mary said with a smile. "Did you bring a horse with you?"

"Well, no, ma'am, I didn't. Will here is going to take me out to the horse auction first thing Monday, and we're goin' to see what we can find. We'll be needin' about six or so horses for the picture, and..."

"But, Twister, you know that you can use Lady and Gypsy and Star, right?" Mary interrupted. "We've already told them they're going to be in the movie!"

Willie cleared his throat loudly in Mary's direction, and Jody elbowed her in the side, but Mary was not to be deterred from her mission of informing Twister of the availability of the three ponies.

"I mean, the ponies are already here on the farm, and Lady and Star have both been to horse shows, where they won first-place ribbons, and Gypsy probably would have too, but she hasn't had the chance to go to a show yet," Mary babbled.

"Oh, I know, ma'am, and as soon as they get that ring done over there we'll try out yer ponies and see how they do. Don't worry, they'll have a chance fair and square. But even so, we'll need a few more horses to round out the bunch."

"Willie, are you really going to a horse auction?" Jody asked quietly.

"I reckon so. That's what we were just talkin' about. I don't know if we'll find anything halfway decent, but it won't hurt to look."

"Don't worry, Jody, if anybody can find a good horse, it's Will. He's got the best eye in the country for horses," Mr. Crowley said reassuringly.

"Well, we'll have a few days to work with them once they get here," Willie said modestly, "so maybe we'll be all right."

Mary and Jody were speechless, still pondering Mr. Crowley's comment about Willie's expert eye for horses. But Jody had one more question to ask.

"Um, Willie, if you and Twister are going to a horse auction, do you think we could go too?" she asked shyly. Then she turned sharply when she heard Mary gasp.

"Oh, my gosh!" Mary blurted, her mouth agape. "I just realized what you said! A horse auction! We've never been to an auction before! I've just read about them in books! Oh, Willie, can we go, please?"

Twister glanced at Willie with eyebrows raised and a half-smile on his face while Willie pulled on his earlobe and shook his head.

"Hmph," Willie snorted, "I'll have to see. Might not be room enough in the truck..."

"Now, Will, you'll have the double-cab truck to use with the gooseneck trailer hooked up. There should be plenty of room for these young ladies," Mr. Gordon said, grinning at the upturned, eager faces of the girls.

"Well, I s'pose it'll be all right, that is if you behave yourselves, and don't run off and git lost once we git there," Willie said, trying to sound grumpy.

"Oh, thanks ever so, Willie! We won't get lost, we promise!" Mary said ecstatically while Jody simply shivered in anticipation.

"Well, girls, how would you like to see what we've done so far in the house?" Mr. Gordon offered generously. "That's where our first scene will be shot tomorrow, and we're just about finished setting up."

Mary and Jody nodded happily and followed Mr. Gordon through the red double doors at the front of the McMurray farmhouse. They had to be careful not to trip over the thick black and yellow cables that snaked along the hallway floor. But when they reached the old, familiar kitchen where at times they had dawdled, talking with Mrs. McMurray at the trestle table, they stopped in their tracks and stared.

More cables, leading to several three-legged, tall, black poles each topped by a large, square light, lay on the wood floor of the kitchen. Thick, yellow plastic sheeting covered each window except the one above the kitchen sink. Several of the blue metal boxes the girls had seen disappearing into the house the day before were sitting along one wall, mostly empty, but a few with more cables and cords inside. Men and women dressed in sturdy denim or khaki shorts and cotton T-shirts bustled about the kitchen, some with rolls of black or multi-colored duct tape hanging from their belts, some with walkie-talkies, and some with large metal clips attached to their

At the kitchen table, in the midst of
all the chaos, sat Mr. McMurray.

shirts. And at the kitchen table, in the midst of all the chaos, sat Mr. McMurray, sipping a cup of tea and beaming like a Cheshire cat at the "movie people."

"Well, what do you think?" Mr. Gordon asked the incredulous girls. "It looks a bit different than the last time you saw it, eh?"

"Oh, my gosh, Mr. Gordon," Jody whispered. "What are all these people doing?"

"They're working, of course!" Mr. Gordon chuckled. "These are the crew members, and they're setting up the lighting and the sound for tomorrow. It takes quite a while to get everything ready for each shot. And once the actors get here in the morning, the crew will have to adjust everything again to get it exactly right."

"The actors? Will they be here tomorrow?" Mary asked excitedly. "Oooh, I can't wait to meet them!"

"Now just hold yer horses and settle down." Willie stood behind them in the doorway with his hat in his hands, gazing around the room in admiration of the hardworking crew members. "The actors have a job to do, and they don't need you two buggin' them to death."

"Only the actors who will be in this particular scene will be here tomorrow, girls," Mr. Gordon explained. "That will be the lead female character and the actors who play her mother and father."

"And you two will be busy takin' a ridin' test, so don't worry about bein' underfoot in here," Willie continued.

"A riding test? What do you mean, Willie?" Mary asked.

"Didn't you hear what Twister said? You and the ponies have to prove yourselves if you want to be in the movie. We'll see you in the ring first thing tomorrow mornin'."

"In the ring? But Willie, they're still building the ring," Jody said. "They won't be done by tomorrow!"

"Won't they?" Willie said mysteriously, turning toward the door. "Come on now. There's still work to be done at the barn. And these people don't need you standing around gawkin' at them."

As the girls turned to Mr. Gordon to thank him for inviting them on the set, they saw Mrs. McMurray bustling down the hallway toward the kitchen, shaking her head and clucking her tongue at the sight of Mr. McMurray sitting at the kitchen table among the crew.

"Shamus! Have you nothing better to do?" she asked, looking down at him with her hands on her hips.

"Oh, Maureen, let me be. How many times will we have a movie made in our very own kitchen?" he chuckled. "And they don't mind. Do you, lads?"

Mary and Jody smiled when the crew members—even the women (who seemed to like being called "lads")—slapped Mr. McMurray's open hand and assured him that they didn't mind. As the girls turned to follow Willie out the door, Mrs. McMurray caught their eye and winked, all the while tsk-tsking in the direction of her gleeful husband.

"I think Mrs. McMurray is having just as good of a time as Mr. McMurray. She just won't admit it," Jody whispered, linking arms with Mary and skipping down the farmhouse steps behind Willie. But instead of heading toward the barn, Willie turned the corner of the farmhouse.

"Where are we going, Will..."

For the third time that day, Mary stopped in mid-sentence, speechless. She and Jody could not believe their eyes when they looked straight across the farm-house yard at the old wheat field.

Where earlier in the day the bulldozer had only just taken the first bite out of the soil and stubble, there now lay a beautiful oval of white sand and rub-ber, perfect footing for a riding ring. And surrounding this, as if by magic, rose a brand new three-board fence with evenly spaced posts and a swinging gate at one end. A crew of men was just putting the finishing touches on the gate, installing little wheels on the bottom so the gate could roll into place and be fastened with a nifty hook over the top of the first post.

"Oh, Willie," breathed Mary in awe, "how could they possibly…"

"I told ya, things happen fast on a movie set," chuckled Willie. "They've got to get it done so they can start filming."

"So that's really where we'll be riding tomorrow?" Jody asked, even though she already knew the answer.

"That's the place," Willie nodded. "Now why don't you get your chores done and get on home. You've got a big day tomorrow, what with meetin' the stars and everything."

Mary and Jody looked up to see if Willie was joking, but he had already turned to head down to the barn for milking. Then they spun on their heels and galloped as fast as they could go to Lucky Foot Stable to tell the ponies all the exciting news of the day.

The Riding Test

MARY AND JODY hardly slept a wink that night, so excited were they to be at the farm bright and early the next day. They both set their alarm clocks for 5 a.m., not quite sure what Willie had meant by "first thing in the morning." But they were sure of one thing: they wanted to be the first to arrive, to show Twister and the rest of the "movie people" that they were hard workers and dependable.

At precisely 5:30 a.m., Mary arrived on her bike at the end of the lane, and it was only a few minutes later when Jody joined her there. (They had promised each other that whoever got to that point first would wait for the other.) Without a word, they pedaled furiously up the gravel drive, their bike tires flinging tiny rocks everywhere in their haste to be the first on the movie set. But when they turned the corner to the McMurray farmhouse, they saw plainly that their plan had been in vain.

Members of the movie crew were already bustling about, carrying equipment to and from the house, calling and whistling to each other as though they had been up for hours. The ThomKats catering truck was open and ready for business, cheerfully handing plates of made-to-order breakfast sandwiches and omelets out the windows to several of the hungry crew members. Others gathered around the breakfast buffet table, helping themselves to oatmeal, eggs and bacon, biscuits and gravy, creamed chipped beef, and all kinds of fresh fruit and juice. And in the midst of it all was Finnegan, wagging his tail, spinning in circles, and panting happily as he received one treat after another from the generously heaped plates.

"Well, I guess we aren't the first ones here after all," Mary said glumly. "What time do you think they all got here, for Pete's sake?"

"You know what Willie said, Mare. Making movies

is a lot of work, and it takes a lot of time. I guess they have to start really early to get everything done that they need to do in one day."

"That's right," came a voice from behind the girls. Spinning around, they were surprised to see Twister, grinning and twirling his handlebar mustache. "The crew started setting up at 5 a.m. They have a certain number of shots they have to get finished in one day. And sometimes it takes longer on the first day, just because they're workin' the kinks out."

Twister grinned even wider when he saw the looks of awe on the faces of the girls as they watched the crew buzzing around like honeybees. "So, are you girls ready for your big ridin' test?" he asked, raising an eyebrow.

"Um, I guess so, Twister. What do we have to do exactly?" Mary asked hesitantly.

"Well, why don't you get yourselves somethin' to eat first, then I'll fill you in."

"Us? Get something to eat? Are we allowed?" Jody asked, licking her lips at the sight and aroma of the steaming trays of food.

"Well, I reckon so, bein's how you're trying out for the movie and everything. And don't worry, there's always plenty of food to go around," Twister whispered, making a grand gesture toward the brimming table.

Having not had time to eat breakfast before they left their houses, it took no more persuading for Mary and Jody to help themselves to the buffet. They filled their plates and, finding a seat on the grass, dug in hungrily while Finnegan rolled, sat up, offered his paw, and whined pitifully until Mary finally gave in and fed him a biscuit.

"That dog's going to be as fat as a pig by the time the movie's done," laughed Jody.

"Hey, I wonder where Willie is," Mary said suddenly. "I guess he must be helping Mr. Mooney and Jimmy with the milking. Do you think he'll still milk the cows every day, even with the movie going on?"

"You know Willie, Mare. He has to be doing something all the time. He'll probably help with the farm work until they need him to be the wrangler."

Just as the girls scraped the last morsels of food from their plates and put them down for Finnegan to lick, Twister appeared from around the corner of the farmhouse.

"I just got a good look at the ring," he announced. "Looks like that sand and rubber is ready for a few good hoofprints to mess it up some. Why don't you girls go down and get your ponies ready and meet me up here as soon as you're done? By that time, Will oughta be here too. We'll just put you through your paces a little bit. Nothin' to worry about, just ride like you always do."

"OK, Twister," Mary said cheerfully. "Come on, Finney, you greedy dog. You need to get away from all this food for a while. We'll be right back, Twister!"

Mary and Jody linked arms and skipped toward Lucky Foot Stable with Finnegan trotting closely behind. But Jody wasn't feeling quite as carefree as Mary.

"Mare," she whispered as they entered the cool stillness of the stable, "what if we don't pass the riding test? We've never had lessons or anything. And we have to ride with saddles in the ring, not bareback. We haven't had a whole lot of practice with the English saddles."

"Jody, don't worry. I don't think we have to be expert riders. We're supposed to be taking riding lessons in our part of the movie, so it's OK if we're not perfect, for Pete's sake. And besides, they're probably going to be watching Lady and Gypsy even more than they're watching us, and they'll be just fine, as always."

Still, Jody bit her lip nervously as she grabbed Lady's lead rope and headed to the big pasture field where the ponies grazed peacefully, having no idea that they were about to take a "test." She didn't feel much better when the ponies were groomed and tacked up and on their way to the brand new ring. In fact, the nearer they led Lady and Gypsy to the riding area, the more nervous she felt. And when they turned the corner of the farmhouse and saw a group of people standing by the gate, her heart pounded so she thought it would fly from her chest.

"Mare, who are all those people?" she said in a panic. "I thought it would just be Twister and Willie watching us!"

"Well, it looks like Willie, Twister, Jimmy, Mr. Mooney, Mr. Crowley, and a couple of people I've never seen before. Don't worry, Jode, you'll be fine. Just pretend it's like the first horse show with Lady. Remember how nervous you were, and you got a blue ribbon!"

"I know, but that was just the obstacle course," Jody began, "and I was riding bareback…"

"Now, shush, they can hear us. Don't look nervous. Always look like you know what you're doing, even if you don't. I read that in a book once."

Jody actually trembled as they approached the group, but as much as she wanted to spin around and run back to the stable with Lady galloping behind, she knew it was too late. Mr. Crowley had already spotted them and had turned with a smile and a wave.

"Here they are, our illustrious riding students!" Mr. Crowley announced to the group. "How are you, girls? And what nice ponies!"

"Thanks, Mr. Crowley. This is Gypsy, she's mine, and that's Lady, she belongs to Jody. We're ready for our riding test!" Mary proclaimed all in one breath.

"Well, that's great!" Mr. Crowley chuckled. "But first I'd like to introduce you to some people you may be working with."

"Oh, OK," Mary said, turning to the three strangers standing by the gate. Jody stood silently holding Lady's reins in one hand, afraid that if she spoke her voice would come out all trembly. It was only when Willie pulled on his earlobe and winked at her that she finally managed a smile.

"Jody and Mary, this is Ms. Edythe Pierson. She will be playing the mother of our heroine. And this is Mr. Gerald Lafferty, who will play her father."

"Pleased to meet you," Mary nodded politely.

"Hi," squeaked Jody.

"And this is Ms. Vicki Beaumont, who is playing their daughter, our main character, the one who will be teaching your riding lessons. They've taken a break from shooting inside the farmhouse to come out and see the ring where the riding scenes will be shot. And to meet you girls, of course."

"Nice to meet you, Mary and Jody. I'll be looking forward to working with you," said Vicki Beaumont, patting Gypsy on the neck.

"So this is Gypsy, and...what's your pony's name again? I missed it the first time," Vicki asked Jody with a brilliant smile. When Vicki Beaumont smiled, her brown eyes crinkled at the corners, and her dimples deepened in her cheeks so that her whole face lit up. Jody suddenly lost her nervousness, responding to the kind voice and the way Miss Beaumont impulsively kissed Lady on the nose right then and there.

"Her name is Lady. But sometimes we call her Lady White Cloud when we take her to a horse show," Jody blurted, immediately sorry for her outburst. After all, Lady had only been to one show, and now everyone would expect her to ride like a show pony in the ring!

"Lady White Cloud! What a pretty name!" Vicki

declared. "I can't wait to see what she can do!"

Jody felt herself blushing deep red at that statement, but before she had time to respond, Mr. Crowley directed the attention of the group toward the farmhouse.

"Oh, and look who's here! We weren't really expecting him today—hey, there, Bryan!"

Mary and Jody spun to see for themselves who Mr. Crowley had spoken to. Their mouths dropped open in shock.

Sauntering toward them with a half-smile on his face and his hands casually stuck in his jeans pockets was Bryan McVey, the young and handsome star of his own TV show, which Mary and Jody watched religiously every Tuesday night at eight o'clock. Stopping in front of Lady and Jody, he cocked his head and grinned, reaching out to rub his hand up and down Lady's face.

"Bryan, this is Mary Morrow and Jody Stafford. They're trying out with their ponies to be in the riding lesson scene," Mr. Crowley said. "Girls, this is Bryan McVey."

Mary and Jody could not seem to shut their mouths long enough to respond to Mr. Crowley's introduction, but Bryan McVey was completely at ease with the situation. He turned from Lady and patted Gypsy on the shoulder.

"Nice meeting you, Mary and Jody," he said with a lopsided grin. "Your ponies are beautiful."

"Thank you. So are you," Mary blurted, then clapped her hand over her mouth and closed her eyes in complete and utter mortification.

Jimmy Mooney shook his head and snorted loudly, and the rest of the group chuckled as Mary turned Gypsy quickly from where she stood, hoping to hide her reddened face. She started to put her foot in the stirrup when she felt a hand take the reins from her grasp.

"What are you doin'?" Willie asked quietly, mindful of Mary's embarrassment. "You can't mount up and just take them into a ring where they've never been before. Now just lead her in and walk her around a couple of times so she can look around and get used to the situation. Jody can follow you in."

Mary nodded silently and gathered up Gypsy's reins, leading her smoothly through the open gate with Jody and Lady following. As they began their walk side-by-side along the rail, Mr. Crowley waved and called out to them as he turned away with the group of actors.

*Stopping in front of Lady and Jody,
he cocked his head and grinned, reaching
out to rub his hand up and down Lady's face.*

"Will and Twister will be taking over from here. We've got to get these people back to work. Good luck, girls. I'm sure we'll see you in the next few days."

"Oh, thank goodness, they're not going to watch us," Jody breathed.

"I can't believe I said that, I can't believe I said that," Mary said miserably, shaking her head. "I just can't believe I said that!"

"Oh, don't worry about it, Mare," Jody said, secretly glad she hadn't been the one to say it. "He probably gets people saying stuff like that to him all the time. Anyway, can you believe it's really him? I almost fell over when I saw him! He looks just the same as he does on TV!"

"I know, doesn't he?" Mary exclaimed, forgetting her embarrassment in the excitement of the moment. "And he actually talked to us! Do you think we'll see him again?"

"Probably, if we get to ride in the movie. That's what we have to concentrate on now, riding well enough and showing off the ponies so we all get the part."

"All right, girls, I think the ponies are OK with the ring." Twister called out as if on cue as they neared the gate for the second time. "Why don't you go ahead and mount up, and we'll see how it goes."

Mary and Jody glanced ringside and were relieved to see that everyone including Jimmy and Mr. Mooney had disappeared, leaving only Willie and Twister. They lowered their stirrups on the left side of the saddles and almost in unison placed their left feet in the irons, swinging themselves neatly onto the ponies' backs. All of the years practicing their circus act together in the big pasture were finally paying off. And now that Jody was seated comfortably on Lady's back, she smiled and sat up proudly, her nervousness gone.

Willie and Twister entered the ring, and Willie closed the gate behind them. Lady and Gypsy stood perfectly still, waiting, as always, for their cue to move forward.

"Just get them on the rail, and let's pick up a trot," Twister commanded.

The girls turned the ponies easily toward the rail and trotted off smoothly, with Lady following Gypsy in the easy rhythm that they were both accustomed to. Mary and Jody started off in a sitting trot and then began rising and sitting to the cadence of the ponies' movements as Willie had shown them on the few occasions he had taken time out from farm work. They trotted on the rail several times around and then changed direction at Twister's request.

"This ring is so nice!" Mary exclaimed over her shoulder to Jody. "I feel like we're floating on this sand and rubber!"

"I know! Do you think we'll get to keep the ring when the movie's finished?"

"Well, I don't think they'll go to the trouble to rip it up!" Mary laughed.

"OK, girls, less talkin', more ridin'," Twister said, trying to sound stern. "Now let's come down to a walk, and we'll try a canter."

"Oh, this is the fun part," Mary said under her breath.

"OK, now, canter!" Twister called out, and the girls only had to nudge gently with their heels to encourage Lady and Gypsy into a nice slow canter, twice around the ring, changing direction once.

"All right, that's enough for now," Twister said, waving the girls to a halt in the center of the ring. Twister stood with Willie in front of Gypsy and rubbed his hand up and down on her muzzle. "Will and me'll talk it over, and we'll let you know tomorrow if you passed or not."

"Tomorrow! But, Willie, can't you just tell us now?" Mary pleaded. "We won't be able to sleep tonight wondering if we made it or not!"

"You can wait 'til tomorrow," Willie replied nonchalantly, "and I betcha a dollar you won't have any trouble sleepin' tonight."

Mary and Jody knew it wouldn't do any good to argue, so they sighed and led Gypsy and Lady out of the ring and down to Lucky Foot Stable, where they quickly untacked, groomed, and turned them out in the big pasture. They gave Star a carrot they had saved from the food table and made sure he had plenty of hay and water in his paddock. Then they climbed on their bikes and, waving goodbye, pedaled in opposite directions toward their homes.

And Willie's prediction turned out to be true. The second their heads hit the pillows that night they were asleep, completely worn out from all the excitement of the day.

Willie's Request

T HE SCENE THE next morning at the McMurray dairy farm looked much the same as it had the day before—crew members bustling about, some lined up at the breakfast buffet, others winding up cables, still others unloading more metal boxes from the big white trucks in the machinery yard. Mary and Jody arrived early once more in anticipation of learning whether they passed the previous day's riding test. After feeding Star in his paddock and promising to come back later and groom him, they made their way up to the farmhouse to find Twister and Willie.

"Mare, what if we didn't make it?" Jody said, biting her fingernails. "What will we do if we just have to watch other people ride? And…" she continued, as a terrible thought came to her, "what if the ponies made it, but we didn't? Then we'll have to watch other people ride our ponies!"

"Jody, will you stop it? Of course we made it," Mary said confidently. "Willie said the girl in the movie teaches lessons for beginners. We're at least good enough for that. It's not like we have to jump or anything. And nobody could ride Gypsy and Lady as well as we can. So stop worrying! And stop biting your fingernails!"

Jody obediently removed her fingers from her mouth, clasped her hands behind her back, and bravely squared her shoulders for the remainder of the walk to the farmhouse. But the second she saw Twister emerging from the corner of the food truck, her anxiety returned, along with her nervous habit.

"Mornin', ladies," Twister said, approaching them nonchalantly with a foil-wrapped sandwich in his hand. "Now what could be makin' you bite your fingernails like that, Jody?"

"Nothing, Twister, nothing at all," Mary replied, grabbing Jody's hand from her mouth and linking arms with her so that she couldn't resume the habit. "Jody always bites her fingernails. It's just something she likes to do."

"Oh, I see," Twister nodded. "Well, I'm fixin' to sit down and eat my breakfast. Wanna join me? Plenty of food up there."

Jody thought she would bust any minute if Twister didn't tell them if they had passed the riding test, but Mary was not about to let Twister think for a moment that they were the least bit anxious.

"Sure, we'll join you, Twister. Go ahead and sit down, and we'll get our plates."

While Mary and Jody made their way to the food line, Twister turned away quickly so they couldn't see the ornery grin that was spreading across his face. Jody took her place in line behind Mary and grabbed an empty plate from the pile at the end of the table before she spoke.

"How can you be so calm? Why don't we just ask Twister if we made it?" she whispered fiercely in Mary's ear.

"Well, maybe Twister wants to wait until Willie gets here to tell us," Mary whispered back. "And I think he just might be testing us to see if we can stay calm under pressure. Appearing in the movies puts you under a lot of pressure, you know," she continued knowingly.

Jody sighed and silently filled her plate, stopping only to throw Finnegan a scrap of bacon. She picked up a glass of juice and followed Mary to the table where Twister sat joking with other members of the movie crew.

"Come on and sit down here, Mary," Twister invited, pulling out the chair next to him. "And Jody, there's an empty chair across from Mary."

"Thanks, Twister," Mary said nonchalantly as she and Jody took their seats. Jody took a forkful of scrambled eggs in her mouth and glanced up at Twister, hoping to read his face for a clue to their futures, but Twister was concentrating very hard on finishing his own egg and biscuit. No one spoke until one of the crew members stood with his empty plate in hand.

"So, I hear you girls are going to be riding for us," he said cheerily. "Congratulations! We'll see you in the ring." And he turned and was gone.

Jody's mouth was already open, a second forkful of eggs about to enter, when the meaning of the man's comment sank in. She dropped her fork and looked again at Twister, who sat back and nodded at her with a huge grin on his face.

"I knew it! I knew it!" Mary shrieked. The other crew members at the table chuckled as they stood with their empty plates, each of them congratulating the girls as they left the table to go back to work in the farmhouse.

"Twister, why didn't you tell us yourself?" Mary gasped. "We were dying to know the whole time!"

"So much for being calm under pressure," Jody mumbled to herself.

"Well, I guess I didn't get the chance, since old loudmouth told you first," Twister said, pretending to be upset. "But anyhow, now you know. And you need to get done with your breakfast and meet Will down at the stable. He's got somethin' to ask you about."

Without another word, Mary and Jody grabbed their half-full plates and sprang from the table, heading for the trash can at the end of the buffet. But Finnegan intercepted them and begged so heartily that they gave the rest of their food to him.

"I swear that dog has gained ten pounds since the movie people got here," Mary muttered as they trotted toward Lucky Foot Stable. "He doesn't even go down to the barn to help round up the cows anymore."

"I wonder what Willie wants to ask us about," Jody said warily. "Do you think he's mad about something?"

"I don't know what it would be! But we'll soon see! Hey, that rhymed," Mary chuckled.

When the girls entered the cool stillness of the little white stable, Colonel Sanders was perched on the top board of Lady's stall. Star hung his head inside the stable from the door to the paddock, nickering to them as if to say, "Hey, what about that grooming you promised me?" But Willie was nowhere to be seen.

"Well, I guess Willie came and went, or maybe he's not here yet," Mary observed. "Maybe he'll be here by the time we finish taking care of Star."

Almost at the same instant the words crossed Mary's lips, Willie appeared in the doorway of Lucky Foot Stable, tugging on his earlobe as he always did when thinking about something.

"Willie! You'll never guess what! We passed the riding test!" Jody blurted even before Willie had a chance to enter the stable.

"Oh, you did, didja?" Willie smiled. "Who woulda guessed it?"

"Jody, of course Willie already knew we passed," Mary said. "He probably had a say in the whole thing."

Willie took a hard brush from Jody's grasp
and began grooming one side of Star while
Jody worked on the other side.

Without a word, Willie walked over to Star and scratched him on the special spot behind his ear. In response, Star rubbed his head up and down, up and down Willie's arm. The girls waited expectantly for Willie to speak, but still he said nothing. It was Mary who finally broke the silence.

"Um, Willie, Twister said you wanted to talk to us about something..."

"...Did we do something wrong?" Jody finished.

Still Willie said nothing, and the girls knew they would just have to wait until Willie was ready to say whatever it was he had to say.

"This colt needs a good brushin'," Willie finally said, hooking a lead rope to Star's halter. Willie opened the Dutch door and led Star in from the paddock, putting him on crossties in the aisle. Jody went to her tack trunk and silently gathered up her hoof pick and brushes while Mary sat on a bale of hay, softly whistling a tune to herself.

Willie took a hard brush from Jody's grasp and began grooming one side of Star while Jody worked on the other side. Willie didn't speak until he had almost reached Star's hindquarters. Then he stopped and rested the brush on Star's back.

"We're goin' to need a couple of good horses to use for a ridin' test," he said.

Mary stopped whistling, and Jody stopped brushing, waiting for Willie's next words.

"So we want to ask you if we can use Lady and Gypsy on Saturday for some other girls and boys to come in and ride. We need a few more riders for the ridin' lesson scene in the movie, so the casting director put out a call for young actors who can ride. Now, lots of times they say they can ride, and they really can't, so we have to watch them just like we did you to see if they're tellin' the truth. We'd like to use Lady and Gypsy because they're nice, quiet ponies, and we don't want anybody gettin' hurt in the test."

Willie resumed brushing. Mary and Jody looked at each other, perplexed.

"So, other kids will be riding our ponies?" Jody squeaked.

"That's the general idea," Willie replied. "Now, it'll just be once or twice around the ring. By that time, we can tell if they can ride or not. We're not lookin' for expert riders, but they have to have a decent seat and be able to steer the ponies around the ring without fallin' off."

Willie picked up a tail comb and gently worked the tangles out of Star's black-and-white tail until it hung straight and shining. Still Mary and Jody didn't know what to say. The idea of other people riding Lady and Gypsy! It was almost beyond their imagination!

"Well, why don't you think about it and tell me or Twister what you decide," Willie said, carefully laying the comb in the top shelf of Jody's tack trunk. He patted Star on the rump and headed for the back doors of Lucky Foot Stable. Just before setting foot outside, he turned.

"The producers said they'd be willin' to pay you somethin' for the use of the ponies," he said. Then he was gone.

★7★

Test Part Two

THE RIDE TO Lucky Foot Stable on Saturday morning was filled with apprehension for Mary and Jody. Even though they were in separate cars, coming from opposite ends of the road, their thoughts were the same, both wondering if they were doing the right thing.

After Willie had asked their permission to use the ponies for the riding test, Mary and Jody had talked it over. First they had adamantly decided against it. Then they thought that maybe they should do it because Willie asked them to (and he never asked for favors).

Finally they reasoned that the money they would earn would help pay for the breeding fee to save Star, meaning Willie wouldn't have to pay for all of it himself. Still, they couldn't fully make up their minds until they went home and talked it over with their parents.

Jody spoke to her father and Mary to her mother, and then the two adults spoke on the phone, and eventually they all came to the same conclusion: Willie needed help, and the girls should do anything they could to help him!

Jody's father and Mary's mother offered to be there for the day since it was a Saturday and neither had to work. They agreed to meet at Lucky Foot Stable at eight o'clock in the morning, an hour before the riding test was to begin. As so often happened when Mary and Jody rode their bikes to the farm, the two cars pulled into the farm lane at almost the same time and then parked side by side outside the back doors of the stable.

Mary and Jody somberly stepped out of their respective cars and then silently walked together into the little barn.

"Good morning, Frank," Mary's mother said, emerging from the car with a smile for Jody's father. "Looks like we have two nervous girls here today."

"Mornin', Katherine. You're right about that. Jody could hardly sleep last night worrying about it. I tried to convince her that everything will be fine. Willie's here to run the test, and he obviously knows what he's doing."

A moment later Mary and Jody appeared from the stable, lead ropes in hand, and turned toward the big pasture where Lady and Gypsy grazed peacefully, unsuspecting of the momentous day ahead.

"May we come along?" Mary's mother asked quietly.

"Sure," Mary shrugged. The two adults shared a glance and fell in step behind the despondent girls. Finally, Jody's father broke the silence.

"Now, look, guys, there's no use moping around," he said. "You've made up your minds, and you're doing the right thing. Willie asked just this one favor, and he's certainly done plenty for you. He'll make sure the ponies are fine. Just think, it might be fun watching the others ride."

"Fun? Dad, please," Jody said grumpily. "Lady and Gypsy won't know what to do with other people riding them. They're only used to us."

"Oh, is that so? Do you think that no one ever rode them before you did? Now I know that you two ride them the very best, but I think they'll be OK for the others. After all, you've trained them to accept any challenge, right?"

"And don't forget how well Lady did at her very first horse show," Mary's mother added. "Nothing seems to bother her. And Gypsy will do just as well, I'm sure."

At that point Mary and Jody were busy opening the gate, so they had an excuse not to answer. The adults watched in silence as the girls headed across the field to catch the two ponies. Suddenly, a voice came from behind them.

"How're they doin'?"

"Willie!" Jody's father turned and shook the hand that Willie offered. "The question is, how are *you* doing? Does all this movie business agree with you?"

"Well, I guess as much as it ever did," Willie replied. "I just hope this ridin' test ain't causing too much ruckus with those two."

"Don't worry, Willie. They're happy to do it. They just don't know it yet," Mary's mother chuckled.

"Well, it won't take too long. We should know pretty quick who can ride and who can't. We want to get started in 'bout a half hour. In the meantime, if you come up to the house with me, I'll introduce you to the director and some of the other people who'll be workin' with your daughters."

Just as Willie finished making this offer, Mary and Jody appeared at the gate with ponies in hand.

"Hi, Willie," Jody said half-heartedly.

"Mornin'," Willie nodded. "Glad to see you two bright-eyed and bushy-tailed this mornin'. Now while you girls get the ponies groomed, I'm goin' to take your parents up to meet Mr. Gordon and some of the others."

"OK," Mary replied listlessly, opening the gate and leading Gypsy through. Jody and Lady followed without a word.

"Oh," Willie said suddenly. "One more thing. You don't have to tack the ponies up."

"Don't tack them up? Why not, Willie?" Jody asked.

"Well," Willie said, scratching the side of his head, "go ahead and put them in their stalls and then follow me up to the house. I have somethin' to show you."

Mary and Jody looked at each other quizzically as they entered Lucky Foot Stable. Once they had the ponies safely in their stalls, they fell in line behind Willie and their parents, following them silently toward the farmhouse. When Willie reached the first of the white trucks parked near the house, he stopped and turned to the girls.

"Now listen. In the movie, the main character is going to be teaching Western lessons. You girls have English saddles, so we can't use them for the riding test."

"Western lessons? But Willie, we've only ridden English since we got our saddles!" Jody exclaimed. "And we rode English in our riding test!"

"Neither one of you will have any trouble ridin' Western after ridin' bareback most of the time. Western is more like bareback than English, anyway. You'll see."

"But we don't have Western saddles!" Mary said, perplexed.

"Oh, yes we do," Willie said. Turning to the truck, he took hold of the bottom of the accordion door and shoved upward. The door slid up easily, revealing a cavernous interior. Curious, the girls moved closer and peered inside. Then they gasped in unison.

Lined up on the right side of the interior wall were a row of evenly placed metal saddle racks. On the racks were five brand new Western saddles, complete with bridles hanging beneath on little hooks. Above each saddle hung a square Western saddle pad, each of a different pattern and color. Mary and Jody gazed open-mouthed at the spectacle until Willie chuckled and turned to their parents.

"We didn't have these in time for the girls' ridin' test. The production company just bought 'em this mornin.' Must be nice to have enough money to spend on somethin' like this."

"Well, girls, what do you think?" Mr. Stafford asked with a smile.

"Dad, they're beautiful!" Jody exclaimed, almost forgetting to be upset about other people riding her pony. "Willie, you'll have to teach us how to put them on. The girths are different from the English saddles."

"First off, it's called a cinch, not a girth, and that's just what I'm about to do," Willie said, stepping up into the truck and pulling a saddle and bridle from the rack. "Mr. Stafford, if you'll handle another one of these, we'll take 'em down to the barn and put 'em on."

"But, Willie, will the ponies mind them?" Mary asked worriedly. "They're not used to them, and how do you know they'll fit?"

"Don't you worry. Western saddles are a lot easier to fit than English, and the ponies will get used to them in no time. I wouldn't be surprised if they've worn them before sometime in their lives. Now let's quit yackin' and get down to the barn. Time's a'wasting, and the ridin' test will be startin' before you know it."

Exactly one half-hour later, Mary and Jody stood at the gate of the new outdoor ring with Lady and Gypsy groomed and tacked up, looking very smart in their new Western saddles. Mary's mother and Jody's father sat on folding chairs outside the ring, chatting as they waited for the test to begin. The girls looked to the right and left, expecting to see a group of would-be riders lined up expectantly, but there was no one in sight.

"I wonder where everybody is?" Jody asked, scratching Lady on the forehead. "Willie said the test is supposed to start at nine o'clock."

"Maybe they're not coming after all," Mary said hopefully. But just as the words escaped her mouth, she spotted Willie coming around the corner of the farmhouse, followed by Twister. Falling in behind Twister, in single file, marched the group of young actors. Jody drew in her breath at the sight of them, and Mary patted Gypsy nervously on the shoulder as they drew near. Willie was tugging on his earlobe, but when he was close enough for the girls to see, he winked at them ever so slightly.

"All right, troops," Twister said, turning to address the group. "Let me introduce you to the people who have made your ridin' test possible today. This is Mary and her pony Gypsy, and this here is Jody and Lady. They are allowin' you to ride their ponies today out of the goodness of their hearts. So let's line up along the rail, and I'll go over the rules."

With that, the group spread themselves out along the ring fence, allowing Mary and Jody to get a good look at them. Mary counted heads silently down the line to the twelfth and final rider and then gasped in astonishment.

It was Annie Mooney! Mary cut her eyes to Jody, whose mouth was open in shock, having seen Annie at the same instant. Annie, paying no attention whatsoever to Mary and Jody, was concentrating on Twister's speech. So the girls had no choice but to do the same.

"Now, we're goin' to have you go in two at a time," Twister was saying in his best voice of authority. "We'll give you a hand mounting up, and then we'll just have you do one or two turns around the ring at a walk, jog, and lope. Make sure all your helmets are fastened right good before you mount up. We might have some of you do a pattern in the ring to show that you can stop and turn. I don't want to see anybody doin' anything dangerous, or you'll be asked to dismount. Any questions?"

Mary and Jody looked from one face to another, noticing that several of the riders seemed even more nervous about riding the ponies than the girls were about having their ponies ridden. The next comment, coming from Willie, showed that he observed the same.

"Now look, if any of you don't want to go through with this, speak up now," he said kindly. "Your parents are waitin' at the farmhouse for you. If you're afraid, or don't feel comfortable ridin', just say so, and you can leave now, no questions asked. We don't want nobody gettin' hurt."

At that, one of the girls in the middle of the group raised her hand and burst into tears.

"I don't want to ride," she wailed. "My mom made me come!"

Twister immediately strode over to the girl and patted her on the back. "It's all right, sweetheart," he said. "It's brave of you to speak up. Now, is there any-body else? Last chance."

The first boy in line looked at his feet and shook his head vehemently. Twister took the hand of the crying girl in his and went to the boy, putting his arm around him, and without another word the three turned and walked toward the farmhouse together.

Willie said nothing for a moment, waiting to see if there were more dissenting members of the group. Seeing none, he opened the gate and addressed the first two riders in line, two girls who looked fairly confident in their jeans and Western shirts.

"Come on in, and let's have you each stand by whichever pony you choose. I want to see you tighten the cinch first and then mount up. You can use the mounting block if you need to."

"I don't need it," the first girl in line sniffed as she took the reins from Jody's grasp. "I mount up all the time by myself." She placed the reins over Lady's head and hastily put her left foot into the stirrup to swing herself up. But the instant her full weight landed in the stirrup, the saddle slipped onto Lady's side, and the girl landed on her rump in the sand and rubber of the ring. After raising his hand to quell the snickers from the group along the rail,

Willie reached down and helped the red-faced girl from the ground.

"That's why I said to tighten the cinch first," Willie said, making a point to speak to the group rather than directly to the girl, saving her further embarrassment.

"It's OK, Lad," Jody whispered to Lady. She adjusted the saddle to where it belonged on Lady's back and stood aside while the girl silently hooked the stirrup over the saddle horn and raised the cinch. Lady simply turned her head and looked at the saddle as if to say, "Now, stay put."

Twister returned to the ring, and once the two girls were seated firmly in the saddles, he instructed them to walk along the rail. Gypsy and Lady walked on as though everything was perfectly normal, causing Mary and Jody to feel a little twinge of jealousy. After all, they expected the ponies to act up just a little with different riders on their backs, not to mention different saddles.

But as the riding test continued with Twister and Willie putting each pair of riders through their paces, the girls had to admit that the ponies were just fine no matter who rode them, even when it was obvious that about half of the "riders" had no clue what they

*The saddle slipped onto Lady's side and the girl landed
on her rump in the sand and rubber of the ring.*

were doing. When it came down to the last few in line, Mary leaned over and whispered to Jody.

"Isn't it funny how you can tell as soon as they walk up to the ponies whether they can ride or not? Willie can tell too. He just tells the scared ones to walk along the rail and then dismount."

But the girls had to admit to themselves that there were a few good riders in the group; three of the girls and two of the boys. Then it was down to the last two in line, one of which was Annie.

"I wonder where she got her helmet," Jody whispered to Mary as they watched Annie fasten the strap of the riding helmet under her chin. Mary squinted her eyes at the helmet, and then she gasped.

"Jode, I think that's my helmet!" she whispered back. "Isn't that my helmet?"

"I don't know, Mare, they all look alike, don't they?"

"No, mine has that little tear in the velvet where Finnegan chewed it. See?"

Then it was Jody's turn to squint, and she nodded when she saw the rip in the back of the helmet.

"Hmph, she could've at least asked me to borrow it!" Mary said indignantly.

"Shhh, they're getting ready to mount up."

Annie strode up to Gypsy with the confidence of someone who had already seen all the mistakes the others had made and was determined not to repeat them. She checked the cinch, found it tight enough, and, putting her left foot in the stirrup, swung herself up.

The girl riding Lady seemed sure of herself as well. Twister had the two of them walk, jog, and lope once around the ring. Although she didn't have the best riding form, Annie held her own, even at the lope.

"Do you think she's ever ridden before?" Mary mumbled.

"If she has, she never told us," Jody replied. "But you know how Annie is with animals. She seems to have some kind of gift or something."

Twister gestured for the girls to halt at the gate and watched as they dismounted. Then he turned and addressed the group.

"That ends the test for today. Mr. Will Riggins and I will get together with the casting director and give our opinion. Before you leave, stop at the house and make sure we have all of your headshots and resumés and other paperwork. You'll be hearin' sometime next week if you were chosen."

The girl who rode Lady handed the reins to Jody, and Annie led Gypsy to Mary.

"Thanks for letting me use your hat, Mary," Annie said, unfastening the helmet and handing it to Mary.

"But, but..." Mary sputtered.

"I know you didn't give me your official permission, but when they said I needed a hat, I ran down and got it from the stable, and I was hoping you wouldn't mind. Thanks for letting me wear it. Gypsy was good."

And with that, Annie turned and was gone.

Before Mary could say another word, Willie was by her side, patting Gypsy on the shoulder. Mary's mother joined Willie in the ring while Jody's father stood outside with his elbows propped on the rail.

"Well, I guess these old plugs did pretty good today," Willie said. "I toldja they'd be fine, now didn't I?"

Jody and Mary looked at Willie expectantly, trying to ignore him calling the ponies "old plugs."

"Well, Willie?" Jody said breathlessly. "Which ones made it?"

"Which ones made it?" Willie repeated. "Now how am I supposed to know that?"

"Well...well...aren't you and Twister supposed to choose?"

"All we do is give the casting director our opinion on who can ride and who can't. Then they go through the pictures and decide which ones look best for the part. You girls were automatically picked because they're your ponies and we know you can handle them. They need three more riders, and then they usually pick at least one extra just in case. We won't know 'til next week."

"Next week? Why does it take so long?" Mary asked.

"Next week'll be here before you know it," Willie replied. "And speakin' of next week, have you asked your parents if you can go to the horse auction on Monday?"

Mary and Jody gasped, realizing that they hadn't asked permission for that trip yet. They turned in unison to their parents and pleaded all at once.

"Can we? Willie said we could go and help him pick out horses for the movie. Twister's going too. We've never been to a horse auction before. Can we go? Please?"

"Hmm," Jody's father said, stifling a grin as he came around to the gate. "I think it would be all right if you stay home tomorrow and get all your chores done. What do you think, Katherine?"

"The same for you, Mary. Your bedroom looks like a tornado went through it."

"We will! We will! We'll come up to the barn in the morning to take care of Lady and Gypsy and Star, and then we'll stay home the rest of the day," Mary exclaimed, while Jody nodded vigorously in agreement.

"All right, then. Meet back here Monday mornin' at nine o'clock sharp. Auction starts at ten," Willie said. "Now I got to get down to the barn. It'll be milkin' time before you know it." And he turned and was gone.

The Horse Auction

AS IT TURNED out, Willie didn't have to worry about Mary and Jody being late to the barn on Monday morning. Their parents dropped them off promptly at eight o'clock so they would have plenty of time to feed the ponies before leaving for the auction. They had just finished filling Star's water bucket when Willie appeared in the back doorway of Lucky Foot Stable.

"You girls 'bout ready to go?" he asked. "The earlier we get there the better. Gives us more time to look around."

"We're almost ready, Willie!" Mary exclaimed. "We just have to put Star's bucket out in the paddock for him. Is Twister coming?"

"He's already at the truck waitin' on us."

"Oh gosh, Willie," Jody suddenly said. "Are we all going to fit in your truck? Mary and I barely fit on the front seat with you! Where's Twister going to sit?"

Willie tugged on his earlobe and chuckled before replying. Then he simply turned and answered Jody over his shoulder as he left the stable. "You'll see," he said mysteriously.

Jody hastily toted the full bucket of water out to the paddock and made sure the Dutch door was fastened securely. Then she and Mary fairly flew out the stable doors and around to the barn hill, where they expected to find Willie waiting at his old red pickup truck. But the truck was nowhere in sight. Without taking time to catch their breath, they ran back around to the stable. Still no sign of Willie or Twister.

"You don't think they left without us, do you?" cried Jody. "Where could they be?"

Just then, the girls heard the deep growl of a truck engine behind them on the lane. They spun around and gasped at the sight of a brand new, shiny black double-cab pickup rumbling down the lane from the farmhouse. Hitched to the truck was a huge silver horse trailer. Twister waved to them from the passenger seat. And behind the wheel, grinning like a teenager, was Willie.

"Oh my gosh! What in the world?" Mary yelped.

"Mary!" Jody exclaimed, grabbing Mary's arm. "That must be the truck and trailer Mr. Gordon talked about the other day! Remember?"

Willie pulled up next to the girls and rolled the window down. Then he opened the door and gestured to the extra bench seat behind the driver. "Well, git in," he said.

Mary and Jody needed no more prodding. Climbing in behind Willie and Twister, they sunk down on the plush gray-and-black seat and marveled at the spacious interior of the truck.

"Willie, is this yours? Where did you get it?" Jody asked breathlessly as Willie steered the big truck and trailer expertly down the lane.

"Well, I wish I could say it was mine," he said. "But it's just bein' rented by the film company so's we can pick up some horses. Pretty nice, huh?"

The hour it took to get to the auction seemed to fly by as the girls savored the beauty of the farm landscapes along the way and the richness of the truck, compared to Willie's rickety red pickup with the deep cracks in the seat. Before they knew it, Twister was pointing at the sign for New London Sales Stable. The words were painted on the side of a white, barnlike building at the end of a large parking lot filled with trucks and horse trailers.

"Here we are," he said. "Pretty crowded today. But I think I see a parkin' space."

Willie pulled the big rig into the parking lot and maneuvered it into a space between two other trucks. Mary and Jody looked out the window and immediately saw two horses being led toward the sale barn. Others were in the process of unloading from the many trailers, and there were people riding horses in the parking lot.

"How many horses are there going to be?" Jody asked, watching as a pair of gray ponies was unloaded from one of the trailers.

"Oh, about two hundred or so," Twister answered nonchalantly.

Two hundred horses! Mary and Jody could hardly grasp the enormity of it all. They stepped down from the truck just in time to see a horse-drawn buggy driven by a man with a long beard enter the lot.

"Those are the Amish," Willie explained as they watched the man drive the horse into a shed where two other buggies were parked with the horses hitched to a long rail. "They still abide by the old ways, and they don't have cars or tractors. They depend on horses to do the farm work and provide their transportation. We'll see a lot more buggies in here by the end of the day."

Mary and Jody were speechless as they walked across the parking lot toward the sale barn. All manner of horses and ponies, mules and burros, and even a pair of llamas were traveling with them to the wide entrance into the building. But once inside the cavernous structure, an even more astounding sight met their eyes. In the first section of the building, to the right and left, on either side of a wide aisle, stood a long, continuous row of horses. Their halters were secured by short ropes clipped to rings on the wall, and their hindquarters faced outward to the aisle. Some were munching on the hay provided in a long trough at their heads, some were stomping or shaking their heads nervously, and others whinnied impatiently to each other.

"Now be careful walking down the aisle—stay right in the center," Willie warned. "Some of these horses are kickers, and there's not much room to get out of the way. We're goin' to walk you through the whole barn, and then I want you to take a seat in the risers along the sale ring. Me and Twister have work to do."

Mary and Jody tried to follow Willie and Twister down the very center of the aisle, but it was difficult not to bump into all the other spectators who were attempting the same route. The awestruck girls, elbowing their way through the crowd, gazed from right to left at the array of horses of all colors, shapes, and sizes. They finally made their way to the end of the barn, where a wide exit opened into an outdoor courtyard. In this long rectangular space were even more horses, these with riders showing off the horses' abilities to prospective buyers. Willie and Twister stopped for a moment to watch, then continued around the corner to the second section of the barn, which looked much like the first, with two rows of horses tied in the same manner. The one difference was in the size of the inhabitants.

In the long row on the left were donkeys, miniature horses, and ponies of all colors. On the right stood the draft horses: Belgians, Clydesdales, Percherons, and Shires, their enormous hindquarters towering above the heads of the girls.

"Oh my gosh, they're huge!" Mary exclaimed. "Look how big their feet are, too!"

"And their heads," Jody marveled. "I think that one's head is as big as half my body!"

"The Amish use them in the fields to work up the ground and harvest the crops," Willie explained. "They hitch them up four across."

"And look how cute the ponies are!" Jody continued, turning to the other side of the aisle. "Oh, Willie, can't we squeeze in next to one of them and pet him?"

"No goin' between two ponies," Willie warned. "But you could pat that one at the very end of the row there."

The pony on the end was the color of butterscotch with a cream-colored mane and tail and odd-shaped white patches on various places over his body. When Mary reached out and patted him on the shoulder, he turned his head as far as his rope would allow and rested his chin in the crook of her arm, gazing up at her with liquid brown eyes.

"Oh, Willie, can't we buy this one?" Mary beseeched. "He's adorable!"

"I knew this was gonna happen," Willie mumbled to Twister. "Mary, we can't buy everything we see that looks cute. We're lookin' for some real specific horses here today, and that ain't gonna be one of 'em."

"Ooh," Mary and Jody cooed, stroking the neck and muzzle of the butterscotch pony. "Well, maybe we'll get something else just as cute."

"Speakin' of that, the sale's about to start. You girls git a seat up in the risers by the ring there, and me and Twister will be along shortly. We have to do some more lookin' around."

Mary and Jody made their way with much of the crowd to the rows of wooden bleacher seats rising along either side of another long, rectangular space, this one inside the building. A thick bed of sand covered the floor inside the space and a four-foot-high fence separated the ring from the potential buyers. Mary and Jody found a seat about halfway up the risers, across from a raised platform where the auctioneer sat.

"Look, Mare, there's a lot of the Amish people here that Willie told us about," Jody observed, looking around at the crowd. "The men all have beards and straw hats and wear black pants and jackets."

"And the women all have their hair pulled back with those little white hats on," Mary added. "Look, even the little girls wear the bonnets."

Before Jody could reply, the girls' attention was drawn away from the wardrobe of the Amish to the voice of the auctioneer.

"Test, test," he said into the microphone and then cleared his throat. Mary and Jody searched the faces in the crowd standing along the ring fence, trying to spot Twister and Willie, but they were nowhere to be seen.

"I wonder if Willie is out back watching the..." Mary began.

"Good morning. Welcome to the New London Sales Stable," the auctioneer interrupted. "We have a big crowd here today, so we'd like to ask that you keep the noise down so we can all hear what's going on. We're going to start today with riding horses, then drivers around noon, and finish up with ponies. In between, we've got a few llamas coming in and a shipment of wild horses from out west. Keep your bidding numbers handy."

"Oh, I wonder if Willie knows he has to have a bidder's number?" Jody wondered aloud.

"I'm sure he does, Jode. I think Willie's done this quite a few times before."

"Now we're going to get started," the auctioneer continued. "If we guarantee a horse to be sound, and you take him home and he's not, you bring him right back here, and we'll take him back. If we say a horse is 'as is,' that means you take a chance on what you're getting. No complaints."

The auctioneer took one last look around the crowd to make sure his message was understood. As if from nowhere, a short Amish man with a long gray beard appeared in the center of the ring.

"I wonder what he's doing there?" Mary wondered aloud.

The auctioneer tapped his gavel and raised his hand. "Let's go. First horse."

The first horse to enter the ring was a short, stocky chestnut in Western tack.

His rider, a thin man with a handlebar mustache wearing jeans and a plaid shirt, reined the horse to a halt opposite the auctioneer's platform. Mary and Jody strained to hear above the din of the crowd as he described his mount to the auctioneer.

"This is a twelve-year-old registered quarter horse, quiet, sound, used on trail rides and in Western lessons. He has all his shots and was just de-wormed. Good for any kid to ride."

The auctioneer repeated the description into the microphone and began the bidding.

"Six hundred!" he shouted. A woman sitting directly across from the girls immediately raised her hand. When she did, the Amish man in the ring hopped in the air and yelled, "Yep!"

"See, she don't know what she's doin'," came a voice from behind the girls.

"Twister!" Mary exclaimed. "We didn't see you coming. Where's Willie? And why doesn't that lady know what's she's doing?"

"Will's standin' down there by the ring so's he can see better. And the woman don't know what she's doin' because she should've waited for the auctioneer to come down a little bit from six hundred before she put her hand up."

Mary and Jody looked at each other, confused by Twister's explanation, but didn't pursue the matter. They were more interested in watching the Amish man hop up and down, shouting "Yep!" each time someone's hand went up to bid. Then, as the bidding continued on the first horse, another horse and rider entered the ring.

"Twister, why are they letting the next horse in before the first one is even sold?" Mary asked as the auctioneer's voice droned on. Three people were bidding on the chestnut quarter horse, and the price was up to eight hundred dollars.

"Makes the sale move along faster. This way people can get a look at the next horse before they start the biddin' on it. It also gives people a chance to see if the horse is going to act up in the ring."

In that instant, the auctioneer's gavel came down with a bang at nine hundred dollars for the quarter horse. But when the gavel came down, the second horse in the ring went up, rearing so high that it seemed he might fall over completely. Mary and Jody gasped along with the rest of the crowd as the rider grabbed for the saddle horn and managed to stay on.

"See what I mean?" Twister said calmly.

"Twister, does that horse belong to the man riding him?" Jody sputtered.

"Probably not. The sale barn has people who ride the horses into the ring. The owners usually just pay the riders to ride in for them. That man's probably never seen that horse before."

The horse was down on all four legs then, and the rider had him under control, cantering him up and down the small enclosure. Although the horse was a nice-looking gray, the bidding started at only three hundred dollars, probably due to his "acting up" in the ring. Still, there were two people bidding, willing to take a chance on him, and the price was steadily going up.

"Twister, isn't it really risky to buy some of these horses for the movie?" Mary asked worriedly. "How do you know they'll be good? Maybe we'll get them home and they'll misbehave like that one just did."

"You're right, Mary. When you buy a horse at auction, it's always a chance you take. The movie people normally wouldn't allow it. But this time they are, and it's all because of Will."

"What do you mean, Twister?" asked Jody.

"Well, they trust him. He's known for having the best eye in the country for horseflesh. If anybody can pick out a nice, quiet, steady horse, even out of this rangy bunch, it's goin' to be Will."

Mary and Jody nodded in admiration, remembering that Mr. Crowley had said the very same thing about Willie.

The second horse was sold for five hundred dollars. As he turned to leave the ring, the auctioneer began the bidding on the third horse, a rather gangly Appaloosa horse with a skinny neck. This time the rider merely nodded to the auctioneer, who simply said, "Good, sound, broke, and ready to go," and started the bidding at four hundred dollars.

Mary and Jody spotted Willie standing at ringside and watched him anxiously as each horse came into the ring. They hoped to see him raise his hand to bid on some of the prettiest ones, but Willie stood stock still, eyeing each horse carefully, his hands in his pockets.

"Twister, what if Willie doesn't see anything he likes? Will we go home empty-handed? What will the movie people do?" Mary asked breathlessly.

"Don't worry, he'll see something. There's over two hundred horses here today. He just hasn't seen nothin' he likes yet."

Just as Twister finished his sentence, there was a sudden commotion at the far end of the ring. Mary and Jody gasped along with the rest of the crowd as the side gate was flung open to allow a whole herd of six horses into the ring at once. But these horses were different from the others. Their manes were long and tangled, and their forelocks hung wildly, covering their eyes. They snorted and pawed, and their nostrils flared as they bucked and kicked around the ring. They were almost all the same dull brown color, except for the largest one, who was nearly black.

"This must be the wild bunch the auctioneer talked about," Twister said with a grin. "Now, watch, here comes a rider in the ring to try to round 'em up and calm 'em down."

Mary and Jody watched with mouths open in amazement as one of the sale barn riders on a small-boned bay horse rode directly into the midst of the chaos. The rider made a "Shhhhh" sound with his mouth as he maneuvered the little bay around the outer edge of the ring, herding the wild horses together until they were settled and moving as one in a unified circle. The herding horse trotted calmly, keeping his head high and his ears forward, gazing curiously at the ragged bunch without the least bit of fear in his eyes.

"All right, boys, what's your pleasure on this group?" the auctioneer asked, tapping his gavel lightly on the tabletop. "Straight off the plains, they are. We're selling them by the piece, take one or all. Two hundred!"

The horses continued trotting in a relentless circle, but no one would start the bidding.

"Come on, boys, they're here for sale. Don't take

Mary and Jody gasped as the side gate was flung open to allow a whole herd of six horses into the ring at once.

much to calm 'em down. They'll be like kittens in no time."

The crowd laughed then, but still no one took a chance.

"One hundred, one hundred apiece. You can't lose at that price, folks," the auctioneer pleaded.

A lone hand went up at ringside. Mary and Jody craned their necks to see whose hand it was.

It was Willie's.

Even Twister gasped this time. "What the..." he began.

"Yep!" the Amish man yelped excitedly, pointing at Willie. But Willie shook his head and simply pointed at the bay herding horse.

"He's for sale, but not yet, we're bidding on the wild herd," the auctioneer said insistently. "What do I hear for the wild ones?"

Still no one bid. Willie raised his hand once again and all in one motion lowered it, pointing his finger at the bay, who was still trotting easily around the wild horses as though they weren't even there.

"All right, then," the auctioneer said in frustration. "We'll let the bay horse go and then we'll sell the others. Keep your eye on them, boys. Look, they're calmin' down already. Six hundred on the bay!"

Willie didn't raise his hand this time. The auctioneer glared at him and then banged his gavel. "All right, then, five hundred!"

Willie simply nodded.

"Yep!" went the Amish man.

"Five fifty! Who'll give five fifty?" A hand went up across the ring, and the bidding began. The auctioneer launched into the bidding at such a rate that it was hard to understand him. Several hands were in the air, all bidding on the bay horse, as the little Amish man hopped up and down with each bid.

"What's he saying, Twister?" Jody whispered. "He's going so fast I can't understand him."

"He's up to eight hundred already," Twister said. "I don't know how far Will's going to go on him."

There were just two people still bidding at nine hundred dollars, and one of them was Willie. The other was a man sitting directly behind the auctioneer wearing a black cowboy hat and a shiny black rodeo jacket.

"Oh, I hope the rodeo man doesn't get him," Jody said anxiously, biting her fingernails.

"Nine fifty!" The auctioneer shouted. Willie nodded.

"One thousand! One thousand! Do I hear one thousand?"

The Amish man spun in a circle, scanning the crowd for another bid. The rodeo man turned questioningly to the man sitting next to him, who shook his head no. The auctioneer asked once more for a bid of one thousand. Then the gavel came down with a bang.

"Nine fifty! To number one twenty-three. Now, I *need* a bid on these wild ones!"

Mary and Jody watched as Willie turned abruptly from ringside. He strode as quickly as he could toward the rear of the sale barn, following the bay horse and rider as they left the ring. In an instant, the girls were on their feet and making their way down the bleachers so as not to lose sight of Willie.

"Hey, wait for me!" Twister grumbled, excusing himself for almost stepping on the woman in front of him as he descended the bleachers in pursuit of the anxious girls.

By the time Mary and Jody pushed their way through the crowd and caught up with Willie in the back alley of the barn, the new horse was nowhere to be seen.

"Willie!" Mary panted, "we watched you buy the horse! Where did he go?"

"Oh, him?" Willie said nonchalantly. "I resold him already."

The girls' mouths flew open in shock at this statement until they saw Twister and Willie exchange amused looks.

"Willie! You did not! Can we go look at him? Please?"

"Well, hold yer horses. We're just 'bout ready to load up and go home," Willie replied, turning toward the sale office.

"Go home?" Jody said, bewildered. "But Willie, you only bought one horse. I thought we needed at least three."

"Well, I bought three others straight from the owners before they even went in the ring. Sometimes you get 'em cheaper that way. And I was able to have a good long talk with the owners so's I'd know what I was gettin'. And I rode each of 'em a little bit out in the back here."

"You rode them? But, Willie, we've never even seen you ride! Why didn't you come get us?"

"Come get you? I didn't have time for no foolishness. Now let me be so's I can go pay the bill."

At that, Willie turned and disappeared into the sales office, leaving the girls open-mouthed in dismay.

"Shut yer mouths, yer catchin' flies," Twister said with a grin.

"But, Twister, we didn't even get a chance to see the others Willie bought," Mary said, disappointed. "I thought we could help him pick them out."

"And I didn't think you were allowed to buy them before they went in the ring," Jody added. "Doesn't the sale barn get upset about that?"

"First off, I don't think Will needed no help pickin' out," Twister replied. "And it's OK to buy them before they go in the ring. The sales barn still gets the commission on them, and they don't mind much because it saves them time. That's three less horses they had to sell in the ring."

Before either girl could ask another question, Willie appeared from the office holding four yellow slips of paper, one for each horse bought.

"We have to show these slips to the man on the way out," Willie explained, "so they know we got the right horses."

"Oh, Willie, can we help lead the horses out to the trailer?" Mary pleaded.

"Please?" Jody added.

"Well, I don't know about that," Willie said, glancing at Twister with a half-grin. "What do you think, Twister? You think they can handle one apiece? Maybe I should take two and you take one, and they can handle one between 'em."

"I think that's a good idea," Twister replied seriously. "After all, we don't know these horses. They could be wild broncs for all we know."

Mary and Jody looked from Willie to Twister, trying to figure out if they were kidding, but their faces gave away no clues. Willie simply turned and headed toward the center aisle of the sales barn, and Twister followed. The girls had no choice but to fall in step behind them. When they reached the end of the first row of horses, Willie stopped and turned to the right.

"Here's the three I bought out back," he said, gesturing to three horses tied closely together. "And the bay is tied just a couple horses down the other way. Now I'll back these out, and then I'll let you girls lead the quietest one to the trailer. Twister can lead the buckskin out first, you girls walk in the middle, and I'll get the other two and bring up the rear."

Willie placed his hand gently on the buckskin's rump. "Hey buddy," he said quietly as he sidled in between the two horses tied next to each other. The slipknot came untied easily in his hand, and he backed the horse out, handing the lead rope over to Twister. The horse blinked at the girls with enormous dark eyes and sniffed Twister's hand like a dog.

"Ooh, he's pretty," Jody exclaimed. "I love his color!"

"All right, now, pay attention," Willie said sternly to the girls. "Here comes your horse. She's a mare."

The mare was slightly smaller than the buckskin and an altogether different color. She was a light gray with darker gray dapples and a dark gray mane and tail. Her delicate bone structure and refined head contrasted with the stocky build of the buckskin, but one thing the two had in common was the large size and gentle expression of their eyes. It was all the girls could do to stand still long enough for Willie to place the lead rope in their eager hands.

"This one's supposed to ride and drive, too. She was a carriage horse in New York City. Now be careful walkin' her through the crowd," Willie warned. "I'm right behind you with Stumpy and the bay."

Mary and Jody tried to turn around to see what Stumpy looked like, but Willie waved them on. "You'll see him soon enough. Get that mare movin' right out to the exit. Stay behind Twister and don't get too close to the horses on either side of the aisle."

The new horses were led smoothly out of the barn and to the exit, where their papers were approved by the guard. The mare walked quietly between Mary and Jody across the parking lot, turning her head occasionally to gaze curiously at the various horses being loaded onto trailers for the trip home from the sale. When they arrived at their own trailer, Willie began giving orders.

"Now, you girls hold the mare and stand back while we load the others. If they all load easy on the trailer, which I think they will, we might even get home in time for milkin'."

The gray mare became a little anxious, turning in circles and nickering softly while Willie and Twister loaded the other three horses. Mary and Jody patted her neck and talked quietly to her until it was her turn to load.

"All right, hand me the mare," Twister said, taking the lead rope from Mary's grasp. The mare quieted down immediately when she saw the other horses in the trailer and stepped up without a hitch when Twister led her on. She settled in easily next to the bay as Twister expertly tied her with a slipknot. Before the girls knew it, the doors were fastened, and they were on their way home.

But they still had not gotten a close look at Stumpy.

New Horses

MARY AND JODY could hardly wait to jump from the truck cab when they arrived at the McMurray dairy farm, and it seemed that the movie crew members were almost as excited as they were. Even before Willie brought the truck to a stop at the double doors of Lucky Foot Stable, a crowd of curious onlookers had assembled there, waiting to see the new horses. Even Mr. Gordon, the director, took a break from filming and stood at the front of the line, standing on tiptoe to try and see into the back of the trailer.

"Willie, they're just as curious as we are," giggled Mary, waving at the crowd with a superior air. "We're lucky. We got to see the horses before anybody."

"Well, we haven't really seen them all yet," Jody said. "What about Stumpy?"

"Nothin' special about him," Willie said nonchalantly. "Just an old, scrubby Mustang."

"A Mustang!" Mary fairly shouted. "Willie, you mean like the wild horses of the West? I just read that book called *Mustang, Wild Spirit of the West*, by Marguerite Henry!"

Willie shook his head and chuckled, braking the truck to a stop just outside the stable doors. He stepped carefully from the truck with Mary and Jody following close behind. Twister emerged from the passenger side and went immediately to the back of the trailer to unload the new horses.

"Well, what did you find, Will?" asked Mr. Gordon, craning his neck to see inside the horizontal openings on the side of the trailer. The horses, only their heads visible, gazed curiously back at the gathering crowd.

"I think I got some nice, quiet ones," Willie answered. "One of 'em ain't much to look at, but he's a real gentleman."

"Willie, is that Stumpy? The one that ain't much to look at?" Mary asked, forgetting her grammar for a moment.

"Yes, yes, that's Stumpy," Willie replied. "Here he comes now."

Twister had untied the gray mare and Stumpy from the rear of the trailer and turned them carefully around so that they could step down easily onto the gravel lane. He stood now on the lane with a lead rope attached to their halters in each hand, waiting patiently for the two horses to sniff the air and look around at their new surroundings. Only when he felt that they were ready did he coax them gently from the trailer by tugging on the leads. The gray mare was the first to step gingerly down from the trailer, followed closely by Stumpy, who looked as though he would follow her anywhere. Only when Twister turned the horses toward Willie and relinquished his hold on the lead ropes did Mary and Jody get a good look at Stumpy.

"Oh, Willie, he's cute!" Jody exclaimed. "He's not as ugly as you said!"

"I didn't say nothin' about him bein' ugly, I just said he wasn't much to look at, and he ain't," Willie replied matter-of-factly.

Only when Twister turned the horses toward Willie and relinquished his hold on the lead ropes did Mary and Jody get a good look at Stumpy.

And Willie was right. Stumpy had rather large ears and very wide-set eyes that looked even funnier because someone had completely shaved off his fore-lock, accentuating his broad forehead. He was a dark bay with just one small white spot in the very center of his muzzle. His back was short and his chest was wide, giving the impression that his narrow hind end didn't really belong to him. To finish the pic-ture, the top of his tail had been rubbed to the point that the dock hair was sticking up at all angles, and his mane was a variety of lengths, causing it to flop over on both sides of his neck with some of the shorter hair sticking straight up in various spots along his crest.

"I can see why his name is Stumpy," Mary observed. "He's put together all funny, and he's hardly taller than a pony!"

"Well, his name is Stumpy only because I named him that," Willie said. "Didn't have a name, as far as I know. Now the gray mare there, she's a looker. We've got to think of a name for her."

"Oh, Willie, can we name her? Please? We'll think of the perfect name if you let us!"

"We'll see, we'll see. Now stand back and let Twister have some room. Here come the other two."

Twister turned the second set of horses to face the rear doors of the trailer, but this time they were anxious to get out as quickly as they could to join Stumpy and the mare. Twister hardly had time to step down from the trailer himself before they were standing beside him, stretching their necks to sniff noses with their new friends.

"Well, you've got three good-looking animals there, Will," Mr. Gordon exclaimed, patting Willie on the back. "And Stumpy looks…interesting. Let's hope they ride well."

"Well, you're always takin' a chance buyin' them at auction," Willie replied. "But I rode three of 'em myself, and I watched the other one in the ring round up some wild horses. I think they'll be all right if we give 'em a chance. And o'course, we only really need three, so one's an extra just in case one of 'em doesn't work out."

"Do these two have names?" asked one of the crew members, reaching out to pat the buckskin on the muzzle.

"The buckskin is Augie, and the red bay is Hoppy. The man said he was named Hoppy because he jumped right over his stall door one day when he was a young'un."

The crew laughed, and Mr. Gordon turned suddenly and remembered that they had a movie to shoot. "All right, gang, let's get back to work. One more interior shot and we'll be wrapped for the day. Will, let me know how these work out. You're riding them this evening, I assume?"

"Yes, sir, Twister wants to give them a try," Willie replied, tugging on his earlobe.

"Good. We're about a day ahead of schedule, so we'll be shooting the first riding scene tomorrow, if all goes well."

Mr. Gordon walked away, followed by the crew, and Mary and Jody immediately turned to Willie.

"Willie, what did he mean by that? The first riding scene? Are we in the first riding scene?"

"Well, I reckon you are. We've got to get these horses ridden and settled in tonight, and we'll have to work with the kids tomorrow morning to get them used to the horses. I was hopin' we'd have a little more time, but we'll just have to be ready. Good thing is, the shot that they're doin' is supposed to be the kids' first riding lesson, so I guess it'll be realistic if they're unsure of themselves around horses they've never seen before."

"But, Willie, do you know which kids they picked to be in the riding scene? Did they tell you yet?"

"No, but I'll find out as soon as we get these horses put in the stable. They said they'd know by today. I'd like to use Lady and Gypsy's stalls, and Star's, too, if it's all right with you girls. I'll have to crosstie Stumpy in the aisle for now, since there's only three stalls."

"We don't mind, Willie. Lady and Gypsy are out in the pasture and Star's in the paddock. But when are you going to ride them? Can we watch? Please?"

Making no reply, Willie turned and walked the mare and Stumpy through the back doors of Lucky Foot Stable, followed by Twister with Augie and Hoppy in tow. Only after the horses were settled in the stalls and Stumpy was standing quietly in the aisle did he turn to Mary and Jody.

"I'm not goin' to ride them, Twister is. And I think you girls should go home and get a good night's sleep so's you'll be ready for tomorrow. Call time is usually pretty early."

"What's call time?" Jody asked, looking puzzled.

"That's the time you have to be on the set to get ready for your scene. Could be as early as 5 a.m."

"Oh, but Willie, it's only six o'clock right now," Mary protested. "We have plenty of time!"

Mary and Jody were not about to leave until they found out if Annie Mooney had been chosen for the movie. Willie, silent once more, turned and simply walked out the back doors of Lucky Foot Stable, leaving Twister behind with the girls.

★ 10 ★
Twister Mounts Up

"TWISTER, WE CAN watch you ride, can't we? Our parents aren't coming to pick us up for another hour at least." Mary and Jody were determined to see which of the new horses were going to appear in the movie.

"I reckon it won't hurt," Twister said. "And since you're so keen on stayin', you can help me get the three saddles and bridles out of the trailer and bring 'em down here to the barn."

"We'll help you, Twister! And we can help you put the saddles on, too. Willie showed us how," Mary said with confidence.

Twister chose to tack up Augie and Hoppy and the gray mare first. Only once did Jody have to ask Twister for assistance with the cinch on Hoppy's saddle. Mary had to think hard to remember how the strap worked on the mare's cinch, but she figured it out without asking Twister's advice. All the while, Star gazed curiously in from the paddock, his head over the Dutch door of the stable, stretching his neck and longing to sniff noses with the newcomers.

"It's OK, Star," Jody giggled. "I know you think we're ignoring you, but we're busy right now! We'll come down and groom you later if we have time."

When the horses were tacked up and ready to go, Twister led Augie from his stall and took Hoppy's reins from Jody's grasp. "I'm goin' to lead these two out of the barn, and Jody, I want you to take Stumpy off his crossties and put him in Augie's stall," Twister instructed. "Then we'll all walk up to the ring together."

"Oh, Twister, do you think I could lead Star up to the ring so he can come up and watch with us? We really have been ignoring him lately!"

"Well, I reckon I can take these two up. Will is meetin' us up there, and he can hold Hoppy outside the ring while I ride Augie. If Mary holds the mare, I guess you can hold Star. It'll be nice to see if these horses get distracted by him or not."

Jody quickly released Stumpy from his crossties and led him into the stall vacated by Augie, and then grabbed a lead rope and attached it to Star's halter.

"Come on, boy! This is going to be fun!"

Jody and Star followed Mary and the mare out of Lucky Foot Stable and up to the ring, where Twister stood with Augie and Hoppy, waiting for Willie to appear. As the girls got closer, they were shocked to see Mary's mother and Jody's father standing by the gate, along with Vicki Beaumont and Brian McVey!

"Mom! What are you doing here already?" Mary gasped. Still embarrassed by the memory of her outburst upon meeting Brian, she avoided looking at him altogether.

"Well, Jody's dad and I had dinner together, and we came up as soon as we were finished. We want to see the new horses too, you know!"

"And aren't they nice!" Vicki cooed, rubbing her hand gently on the mare's muzzle. "What's her name?"

"Oh, we haven't named her yet!" Mary replied, suddenly remembering that they had to come up with a suitable name. "Let's think!"

"Wow, this guy's handsome," Brian said, turning to Star and scratching him on the forehead. "Is he going to be in the riding scene?"

"Oh, no," Jody squeaked, blushing. "He's too young. We just brought him up here so he could see what's going on."

"I know the perfect name for her," Vicki whispered to Mary, as if it were their own little secret. "I think she has an exotic look, with her dark-rimmed eyes. How about Shalimar? I always wanted to name a horse Shalimar."

Mary was silent for a moment, thinking to herself that Shalimar didn't sound much like a Western horse, but she wasn't about to disagree with Vicki Beaumont. "I think it's beautiful," she whispered back, patting Shalimar on the shoulder.

Willie suddenly appeared ringside, holding a half-folded piece of paper in his weathered hands. He pulled on his earlobe and then took off his hat and scratched the side of his head.

"Willie, what's that?" Mary asked, cutting her eyes to the paper and trying to see what was listed there. "Is that the list of people who got parts in the riding scene?"

"Now, don't be so nosy," Willie admonished, folding the paper over once more so that the names could not be read. "I'll read them off after we watch these horses go around."

Mary was busting to see the names on the list, but she knew that Willie would only share them in his own good time, so she turned her attention to the matter at hand, watching Twister ride the new horses.

Willie silently took Hoppy's reins from Twister's hands and stood back when Twister placed his boot in the stirrup and swung up on Augie. The big buckskin stood quietly, gazing curiously around the ring with his enormous eyes. Suddenly a shrill whinny sounded from the direction of Lucky Foot Stable. Augie and Star both responded at the same instant by stretching their muzzles to the sky and whinnying back.

"I guess old Stumpy don't like bein' left in the barn by himself," Willie chuckled. "He misses his buddies already, and they only just met."

Twister gathered the reins in one hand and nudged Augie forward with his boot heel, focusing the quarter horse's attention away from Stumpy and back on the business of riding. From then on, Augie responded only to Twister. Jogging and loping smoothly around the ring in both directions, the stocky buckskin never took a bad step. Twister reined him in and grinned widely at Willie.

"Looks like you got a champ here," Twister said admiringly. "He sure knows what he's doin'. Quiet, too."

Willie simply nodded. Twister dismounted and handed Augie's reins to Willie, taking Hoppy's reins all in one motion. In an instant, he was putting Hoppy through the same drill, jogging and loping both directions of the ring. Hoppy cooperated almost as well as Augie but shook his head up and down several times, chomping on the bit. Once, he even threw his head down, almost pulling the reins from Twister's hand.

"This one might need a hackamore," Twister commented after reining him to a stop. "He don't seem to like the bit much."

"Man was ridin' him with a bosal in the ring," Willie acknowledged. "Must be what he's used to."

"What are they talking about?" Jody whispered to Mary, never having heard such words before.

"I don't know, but I can't wait to go home and look them up," Mary replied gleefully.

"They're words for different kinds of Western bridles," Vicki offered, having overheard the conversation. "I had to learn them myself so I could sound like an actual Western riding instructor. I've been doing a lot of horse research. I'll be in the ring with you girls tomorrow, so if I say something wrong, let me know, OK?"

Mary and Jody simply grinned and nodded, flabbergasted that the famous Vicki Beaumont was actually asking for their advice.

"All right, ready for the mare?" Willie asked Twister. Then he turned to the girls. "Have you come up with a name for her yet?"

"Yes, Willie. Her name is Shalimar," Mary responded grandly.

"Shalimar? Who ever heard tell of a crazy name like that for a Western horse?" Willie harrumphed.

"Um, Willie, Miss Beaumont came up with it," Mary replied. Vicki smiled and winked at her as the other adults stifled grins.

"Oh, well, I reckon it's OK, then," Willie replied, pulling on his earlobe in embarrassment. "But I'm goin' to come up with a nickname for her right quick."

"That's fine, Mr. Riggins," Vicki grinned. "I know Shalimar is kind of a silly name, but I always liked it."

Vicki smiled and winked at her
as the other adults stifled grins.

Willie simply nodded as Twister mounted up on the gray mare and put her through her paces around the ring. She was a little spooky at first, eyeing the audience at ringside warily and side-stepping when Finnegan suddenly flew past the ring, barking at a squirrel.

"That's the fastest I've seen Finney move in awhile," Mary commented wryly.

Twister spoke quietly to the mare, rubbing his hand along her neck as he urged her gently forward. Responding to his voice and touch, she soon settled down and loped easily around the ring, coming down from the lope with just a gentle tug on the reins.

"This one's a little worried, but I think she'll be OK once we get her used to the ring," Twister commented as he dismounted. "I think these three will do all right."

"What about Stumpy?" Mary asked. "You didn't ride him yet, Twister."

"I'll get around to it," Twister replied nonchalantly.

"Mary, we have to get home," Mary's mother chided. "Frank and I both have to work tomorrow, and you girls need to get to bed."

"That's right, Mrs. Morrow," Willie interjected. "I was just told that the call time is 6 a.m."

"Oh, Willie, I almost forgot! You didn't tell us who is in the riding scene yet!" Mary blurted.

"Hold yer horses, hold yer horses," Willie answered, taking the folded piece of paper from his pocket. After carefully smoothing the wrinkled missive against his jeans, he raised it to his face and squinted as he read it over to himself. Mary jiggled impatiently but knew it was no use hurrying Willie when he didn't want to be hurried.

"Well, we've got five names here and one alternate," Willie said.

"Nerve-wracking, huh?" Brian McVey said to Mary, nudging her with his elbow. Mary responded by blushing beet red.

"At the top of the list we have the names of Mary Morrow and Jody Stafford," Willie announced. Mary and Jody grinned, and their parents smiled at them proudly.

"We already knew we made it, Mom," Mary whispered.

"And then we have Jeffrey Hunt, says he likes to be called Jeff," Willie continued.

"Oh, a boy," Jody grimaced.

"And then, Jenna Day."

Mary and Jody looked at each other, remembering

that Jenna Day was the girl who forgot to tighten the cinch.

"And last in the main group, Krystal Warren."

"I don't remember who that is, do you?" Jody whispered to Mary.

"No, we'll probably remember her when we see her," Mary replied.

"And an alternate," Willie looked up from his paper and then down again.

"The alternate is Annie Mooney."

★ 11 ★

Annie Has Trouble

MARY AND JODY hardly slept a wink that night, so worried were they that they might oversleep and miss the 6 a.m. call time. They tossed and turned, waking up each hour and staring at their alarm clocks before falling into a brief and fitful sleep. Mary thought about calling Jody on the phone, but she was afraid Jody would be asleep, and she didn't want to wake her. Down the road, the same thoughts were occurring to Jody. When her alarm finally sounded at 5 a.m., she jumped from her bed like a shot. Mary didn't even wait for her alarm to ring. Her feet hit the floor at 4:55, and she lingered by the bed only long enough to turn it off.

At precisely 5:45, Mary and Jody were inside Lucky Foot Stable, having led Lady and Gypsy in from the big pasture, and were grooming them meticulously in anticipation of their big day. Star nickered impatiently from the paddock as if to say, "Hey! Why isn't anybody paying attention to me?"

"Star, I promise, as soon as we finish this movie scene, I'll take you out for a nice long walk, up to the pigeon house and back," Jody called, concentrating on a particularly tough knot in Lady's mane.

"Jody, can you believe Annie is going to be the alternate?" Mary blurted. When the names were announced the day before, Mary and Jody had made no comment, but Mary just couldn't hold her tongue any longer.

"No! I honestly don't think she ever rode a horse before the riding test. Maybe they picked her because of her red hair."

"Ain't you got those ponies tacked up yet?" Willie called suddenly from the back doors of Lucky Foot Stable. "They need to be up to the ring in fifteen minutes."

"We know, Willie, we're almost ready," Jody replied, forgetting about Annie Mooney long enough to throw a saddle pad on Lady's broad back. Mary was a little ahead in the tacking up process, having already tightened the cinch on Gypsy's new Western saddle just the way Willie had shown her.

"Willie, where are the other horses?" Jody asked, lifting Lady's bridle from the peg on the wall. "They weren't in the stable when we got here."

"Twister's got 'em up at the ring already," Willie said. "We were in here groomin' an hour ago so's we could make room for your old plugs to come in."

Mary and Jody were too busy putting the bridles on to take offense at Willie calling the ponies "old plugs." Mary looked up just long enough to notice Willie tugging on his earlobe, the way he always did when about to say something important.

"Willie, what is it? Do you want to tell us something?" Mary asked curiously.

"Well, I just want to remind you that it's goin' to be a long day, and you better get ready to do things over and over again. It's not like ridin' for fun, ya know."

"Oh, we know, Willie. You told us that already," Jody said nonchalantly, leading Lady toward the stable doors and followed closely by Mary and Gypsy.

"And one more thing," Willie said, not moving from his position near Gypsy's stall. "I don't want to hear no remarks behind anybody's back about anything at all, especially about anybody's ridin' ability."

Mary and Jody stopped in their tracks and looked at each other in silent understanding before turning to Willie. "We know, Willie," they said in unison, and then turned and continued on their way to the brand new ring.

Inside the ring, Hoppy stood with his halter fastened over his bridle, a lead rope securing him to a fence post inside the ring. His head was turned just far enough to watch the other two horses going through their paces. Twister was mounted up on Augie, walking him along the rail and leading the gray mare behind. Stumpy, an alternate just like Annie, stood quietly away from the ring, tethered to the lowest branch of the old horse chestnut tree. And standing next to Stumpy was Annie's brother Jimmy, one arm looped over Stumpy's neck, chewing on a piece of straw. When Jimmy saw Jody and Mary approaching the ring, he turned and smirked at them.

"I guess you think you're movie stars now," he snorted.

Mary and Jody chose to ignore this statement by striding past Jimmy to the gate to await Willie's instructions.

"You girls can go on in, but stay on the far side of the ring and be quiet around those other horses. Go ahead and mount up, and walk on the rail and get Lady and Gypsy warmed up."

"But, Willie, where are the other riders?" Jody asked, looking around as she tightened Lady's cinch.

"They ain't here yet," Willie replied as if Jody should have known. "We got to get these horses warmed up and ready to ride before they get here. Their call time ain't 'til seven o'clock." Willie replied.

"Seven o'clock? But that's almost an hour away!" Mary grumbled.

"What's the matter, didja have to get up too early?" Jimmy sneered from just outside the ring, where he had quickly placed himself the moment Mary and Jody entered the gate.

"Don't you have to go milk the cows or something?" Mary retorted, swinging her leg over Gypsy's back.

"Yeah, as a matter of fact, I do. Some people have to do a little work around here." Before Mary could open her mouth in reply, he turned and was gone.

By the time the other riders arrived at the ring, Lady and Gypsy were thoroughly warmed up, and the crew had set up the camera and other equipment, being very careful not to spook the horses. Augie, Hoppy, and Shalimar stood next to Twister and Willie, lazily switching their tails at flies, ready for the first shot. The three actors, two girls and a boy, and Annie Mooney, the alternate, bided their time outside the ring, awaiting Willie's instruction. But before addressing the group, Willie approached Mary and Jody, tugging on his earlobe once again.

"What now, Willie?" Jody asked. "You look worried about something."

"Well, I'm just gettin' an idea," he said. The girls waited patiently to hear what the idea might be, but Willie said nothing. Finally Mary spoke up.

"What kind of idea, Willie?"

"Well, I'm thinkin' it might be best for the scene if you two girls rode these new horses and let a couple of the others ride Lady and Gypsy," he said.

Mary and Jody were dumbfounded for an instant, their mouths hanging open in disbelief.

"Now, shut yer mouths, yer catchin' flies," Willie said, repeating one of Twister's favorite phrases. "The point is, I know for a fact that Lady and Gypsy will behave themselves, and I'm fairly certain these new horses will too. But I know you girls could handle it if one of them decides to act up a little. I don't know enough about these other riders to know if they could handle any horse problems."

Mary and Jody closed their mouths and looked at each other, suddenly feeling very proud that Willie had so much confidence in them.

"Well, Willie, if you think that's best, we can ride the new horses," Mary volunteered.

"Oh, Willie, can I ride Shalimar?" Jody pleaded. "I think she likes me."

"I'll ride Hoppy!" Mary fairly shouted. In their excitement, they almost forgot to be upset about other riders handling Lady and Gypsy.

"Well, that didn't take much talkin' into," Willie mumbled to Twister. He didn't mention the other reason for switching horses. The movie scene called for riders taking their first few riding lessons on horses they hadn't ridden before, and he thought that Mary and Jody would look much too comfortable on their own ponies.

"Well, then, I reckon those two horses would be a good fit for you two," Willie agreed. "Now let's get started."

Willie and Twister turned to the group by the rail. "You kids can come on in," Twister instructed, "except Annie, if you don't mind, stay just outside the gate and listen."

Annie, who was already halfway through the gate, nodded and turned back, propping her arms on the top board of the ring fence. Mary and Jody glanced at each other, almost feeling sorry for her.

"Now, we're goin' to assign your horses to you," Twister announced, "and then we'll take a few turns around the ring until you're comfortable on your mount. Remember, this is supposed to be one of your first riding lessons, so try not to look too good. I know all of you can ride, but this ain't the time to show off your abilities. Just think back to when you first started ridin' and try to imitate the way you did it back then."

"When I call your name, step up and take your horse's reins and lead them away from the group, but don't mount up until we tell you to," Willie continued. "First, let's have Jenna Day ride Lady."

As excited as Jody was about riding Shalimar, she still felt a sudden twinge of anxiety when Jenna Day took the reins from her hands. It was just too strange that someone else would be riding her pony!

"And Jody Stafford will ride Shalimar," Willie announced immediately, noticing Jody's dismay and trying to take her mind from it quickly. Jody smiled bravely as she took the reins from Willie's grasp.

"Jeff Hunt will be riding Augie," Twister continued, handing the reins over to the boy, who smiled and patted Augie vigorously on the neck before leading him off.

"Mary Morrow, your mount is Hoppy," Willie said, leading Hoppy a few steps toward Mary. At the same time, he announced the last rider.

"And last but not least, Krystal Warren will be up on Gypsy."

At the same instant Willie surrendered Hoppy's reins to Mary, Mary handed Gypsy's reins to Krystal, therefore not giving Mary any time to have second thoughts about someone else riding her pony.

"Now that everybody has the correct mount, we'll come around and tighten your cinches, and then we'll get started. Miss Beaumont will be here shortly, and then we'll start shooting the scene, so we don't have much time to get used to our horses."

Although Willie didn't say so, his intention was exactly that. He didn't want the riders to get so comfortable on their mounts that they would look too practiced for the "beginner rider" scene.

Cinches were tightened, and riders were instructed to mount up. Mary and Jody both had a bit of trouble putting their left feet in the stirrups, as Shalimar and Hoppy were quite a bit taller than the ponies they were accustomed to. But determined not to ask Willie for help, they struggled until they were both seated firmly in their saddles along with the other riders. Twister and Willie silently surveyed the group for a moment, and then Twister began giving instructions.

"All right now, let's put Jeff and Augie in front, and the rest of you fall in behind. Walk your horses along the rail single-file twice around and then we'll pick up a slow jog."

Mary and Jody grinned at each other, each knowing what the other was thinking. It was a new sensation, riding a horse rather than a pony! It was certainly further from the ground, and almost scary! To keep from glaring at the girls up ahead riding Lady and Gypsy, they focused all their attention on their own mounts, waiting for the next command, which came a little sooner than expected.

"Now, let's jog," Twister instructed loudly. The group of riders picked up the jog almost in unison.

"Go ahead and let yourselves bounce some," Willie called. "Remember, you don't really know how to ride at this point. You can let your reins have a little slack, too."

Jody was having no trouble "letting herself bounce," as Shalimar's jogging gait was much rougher than Lady's. Up ahead, she could see Mary having the same trouble on Hoppy. Just when she thought her teeth might jounce out of her head, Twister gave the command to walk.

"Good job, everybody," Twister said. "Let's walk to the gate and halt in a straight line across the ring."

Turning Shalimar's head toward the gate, Jody looked up to see Miss Vicki Beaumont standing between Twister and Willie in the center of the ring, looking beautiful in light-tan jeans and a white riding shirt. Jody turned silently to Mary and pointed, trying not to be obvious, but Mary had already seen the actress, as had the other riders, all of whom had grins on their faces as they brought their horses to a halt.

"Good morning, everyone," Miss Beaumont smiled brilliantly and waved. "Oh, there's my favorite horse!" she continued, striding directly up to Shalimar and stroking her neck. "How does she ride, Jody?"

Twister and Willie silently surveyed the group for a moment, and then Twister began giving instructions.

Jody nearly fell from Shalimar's back in shock when Vicki Beaumont called her by name, but she recovered in time to reply.

"She rides fine, Miss Beaumont. She's really good, actually."

"I knew she would be. And Mr. Riggins, have you gotten used to her name yet?"

"No, ma'am, I just call her Sally," Willie replied, scratching the side of his head.

At this statement, Jody and Mary giggled until Willie glared at them, prompting them to cover their mouths and try and look serious. They were saved by the appearance at ringside of Mr. Gordon, the director.

"Are we about ready to shoot, Will?" he asked.

"I believe so, Mr. Gordon. We don't want to rehearse too much and wear everybody out. We're ready whenever you are."

"And I'm ready, too," Miss Beaumont called, patting Shalimar one last time and giving Jody a wink.

"All right, then," Twister began. "Everybody dismount and stand next to your horses. The first scene starts with Miss Beaumont giving instructions on how to mount."

But there was no time for mounting instructions. The instant Mary and Jody touched their feet to the ground, the quiet morning air was split with a blood-curdling scream! The girls looked up in alarm toward the sound of the shriek and covered their mouths in shock. Stumpy was galloping at full speed across the field toward the road. His rider, desperately hanging on with both hands to his mane, dangled with one leg over his back. When Mary and Jody saw red pigtails flying in the wind, they knew the rider was Annie Mooney!

Willie to the Rescue

TIME SEEMED TO stand still in the center of the ring. Riders and crew members stood frozen to their spots, their mouths open in fright. The horses flung up their heads and pricked their ears in the direction of the sound. Only when Willie jerked Hoppy's bridle reins from Mary's grasp did she turn away. And what she saw in the next moment shocked her almost as much as the horrible sight of Annie dangling from the saddle.

Willie, suddenly as agile as a schoolboy, flung the reins over Hoppy's head and vaulted from the ground onto the saddle without using the stirrups. Laying the left rein firmly against Hoppy's neck, in one swift motion he spun the horse in a circle and flew out of the gate in pursuit of Stumpy, who was rapidly approaching the paved road.

"Twister!" Mary screamed, turning to the wiry wrangler. But Twister was already up on Augie and headed out the gate. Knowing that galloping directly behind Stumpy would only make him run faster, Willie was making a wide circle to the right in an attempt to come around in front of the runaway horse. Leaning over the saddle horn, his hat long blown off and hands forward like a jockey, he kicked Hoppy frantically with his heels with each stride. Understanding Willie's strategy, Twister bore to the left, hoping to head Stumpy off if he suddenly galloped in that direction to avoid Willie.

"I think he's gaining on them!" Jody squeaked, clutching Mary's arm with a grip like iron. Mary, too anxious to speak, simply stood with her hands on either side of her face, fixated on the scene unfolding before them. Vicki Beaumont, the color completely drained from her face, put her arm around Mary's shoulder and squeezed.

Willie drew near enough to Stumpy's flank to fling his arm around Annie and pull her to safety.

"Get the set medic!" Mr. Gordon yelled to one of the production assistants. "Have her standing by in case the girl is hurt."

Indeed, it looked as though Annie would fly off at any second if Willie didn't get to her in time. But Hoppy *had* gained on the galloping horse, and just as it seemed that Annie could hold on no longer, Willie drew near enough to Stumpy's flank to fling his arm around Annie and pull her to safety. Hoppy, feeling the extra weight on his side and the tug of Willie reining him in at the same instant, seemed to instinctively know to come down quickly to a halt, allowing Willie to set Annie's feet gently on the ground, where she immediately crumpled into a heap.

The instant Annie landed on the grass, Mary and Jody recovered from their paralysis and grabbed Lady and Gypsy's reins from their hapless riders.

"I'll hold Shalimar!" Vicki Beaumont volunteered, as Jody and Mary vaulted onto their ponies and took off cantering across the field toward Annie. Several production assistants, along with the medic, began running on foot in the same direction.

Willie, having sprung from Hoppy's back an instant after lowering Annie to the ground, kneeled in the grass next to her. As if sensing something wrong, Hoppy stood quietly at Willie's elbow, extending his muzzle toward Annie's still body. Mary and Jody reached the scene just as Twister rode up on Augie, leading Stumpy alongside.

"Is she hurt, Willie? Annie, are you all right? Can she hear me?" Mary gasped all in one breath.

"Twister, ride to the cow stable and get Roy," Willie said, ignoring Mary for the moment. "Just turn Stumpy loose. He'll find his way back to the stable."

Twister did as he was told, releasing his hold on Stumpy's reins and turning Augie swiftly toward the dairy barn. But when Twister galloped off on Augie, Stumpy decided to stay exactly where he was, near Hoppy, where he seemed to feel safe. In fact, horses and people were so thick around Annie that the medic could scarcely get through.

"Please stand back," she implored, setting her black leather bag on the ground next to Annie, who laid still, her eyes closed. The medic took a small white vial from the bag, broke it in half, and held one half under Annie's nose.

"Wow, that must be smelling salts, just like they use in the movies," Mary marveled. "I didn't know they used that in real life."

The smelling salts had just the desired effect on

Annie. She shook her head from side to side, and her eyes flew open. She gazed at the gathering crowd in confusion for an instant and then tried to sit up.

"Wait a minute, honey," the medic said gently, cradling Annie's head in her hand. "Don't sit up yet. Does anything hurt? Tell me where it hurts."

Annie didn't speak but continued looking dazedly at the medic.

Suddenly, "Annie!" came a panicked voice from behind Willie. Mr. Mooney knelt beside his daughter and put his arms out to her.

"Daddy!" Annie whimpered, flinging her arms around his neck. "Stumpy ran away, and I fell off, but Willie saved me!"

The crowd around Annie breathed a sigh of relief as she spoke, realizing that she was at least thinking straight. The medic held the palm of her hand on Annie's back, supporting her as she hugged her father tightly.

"Annie, I need you to listen to me for a minute," the medic said firmly. "Are you feeling dizzy at all?"

Annie simply shook her head no.

"Then I'd like to see if you can stand up, slowly, with your daddy helping you on one side, and I'll be on the other."

This time Annie shook her head yes. Ever so slowly, with the medic supporting her elbow on the right and Mr. Mooney with his arm around her waist on the left, they raised Annie to her feet. The minute she stood upright, the crowd around her burst into applause. At the sudden outburst, Stumpy and Hoppy raised their heads in surprise, but neither moved from their spots.

"Look at the horses," Jody giggled. "They've probably never heard applause before."

But Mary was too busy gathering information to notice what the horses were doing.

"Annie, what happened? Why did Stumpy take off? Were you trying to ride him? Did something spook him?" she blurted all in one breath.

"Leave her be," Willie warned in his *you'd better mind me* voice. "Annie needs to rest right now, and you need to git your horses back over to the ring. We got a movie to shoot."

The no-nonsense tone in Willie's voice was enough to inform not only Mary and Jody, but the rest of the crowd as well, that it was time to get back to business. Almost in unison, the crew, production assistants, and even Mr. Gordon the director turned and headed back to the ring. Mr. Mooney and the medic, with Annie between them, made their way to the stone farmhouse rather than the house trailer so that Annie could lie down and rest in comfort without little Heath bothering her.

At that very moment, Heath was sitting in the middle of the living room floor in the house trailer, playing intently with his blocks. Annie's brother Jimmy sat fidgeting on the couch, watching Heath. But, although Jimmy was watching his little brother, he was not really seeing him. The only thing Jimmy could picture in his mind was the sight of his sister flying across a field, hanging onto the side of a horse for dear life.

And it was all his fault.

Shooting the Scene

AFTER THE TERRIFYING incident with Stumpy and Annie, getting back to the business of making a movie proved to be a more somber affair than Mary and Jody anticipated. They were dying to say something to Willie about his heroic ride, but they could tell from his expression that he was in no mood for conversation. After settling Stumpy in a stall at Lucky Foot Stable, Willie and Twister assembled everyone once again inside the ring. The cameraman and crew took their places. Vicki Beaumont handed Shalimar over to Jody and placed herself in the exact spot in the center of the ring where Mr. Gordon had instructed her to stand. Finally, all riders were lined up in the same sequence as before, standing next to their mounts. It was only then that Twister addressed them, but not in his usual joking manner.

"Now, we've got to concentrate on what we're doin' and put what just happened out of our minds," he said, twisting his handlebar mustache between his thumb and finger. "I don't know what caused Stumpy to run off, and I don't know why Annie was on him at the time, but her daddy's takin' care of her in the farmhouse, and she's fine. Now just remember that you all are inside the ring, and you know your horses are as dependable as they can be. So there's nothin' to be afraid of. Is there anybody that doesn't feel comfortable mountin' up?"

The riders stood silent as stones, no one making a sound.

"All right then, we'll get started. It's goin' to be a long day, but we'll make it as short as we can, if everybody cooperates. Now as I told you before, this scene is s'posed to be your first ridin' lesson. Miss Beaumont is playin' a character named Jenny who has decided on her own to use her family's horses to teach lessons so's she can help with the expenses on the farm. So you all just do as she says, just like a real lesson. When the scene starts, she's already demonstrated how to mount, and she's goin' to ask you to mount up just like she's just shown you. And don't forgit, try not to look too good, even though you know how to ride."

Twister paused and then turned to Willie. "Will, you got anything to add?"

"I reckon not," Willie said, tugging on his earlobe. Although the other riders didn't know Willie well enough to sense anything amiss, Mary and Jody could tell that he was still upset from the incident with Annie.

"All right, then, I'll turn it over to Mr. Gordon."

As if from nowhere, a man wearing headphones and carrying a long pole topped by what appeared to be a stuffed, gray, fuzzy stocking appeared and took a position near Miss Beaumont.

"What in the world is that thing?" Jody whispered to Mary.

"Oh, that picks up the sound," Mary replied matter-of-factly. "I think it's called a boom. I saw Willie with it yesterday. He was holding it over the horses' heads and moving it around so they wouldn't be scared of it when the time came."

Before Jody could reply, two women, one carrying a blue canvas bag with all sorts of pockets and zippers, and the other with a brown leather bag slung around her waist, suddenly trotted through the gate. Approaching Vicki Beaumont with a business-like air, the woman with the blue bag dipped a stubby, round makeup brush into a container of powder that she took from one of the many pockets. First shaking it gently to rid it of the excess powder, she began dabbing the little brush swiftly over the beautiful face of Vicki Beaumont. At the same time, the woman with the brown leather pouch had retrieved a comb from its depths and was concentrating very hard on making sure that not one little hair was out of place on the nape of Miss Beaumont's neck. Mary and Jody watched this procedure with open-mouthed fascination.

"Wow, Jode, it's just like in the movies!" Mary exclaimed in a whisper from the side of her mouth.

"Mare, in case you hadn't noticed, this *is* the movies," Jody said patiently, almost giggling at Mary's awestruck expression.

"All right, last looks, last looks," Mr. Gordon shouted from his seat next to the monitor, a sort of television where he could watch the action unfold just as it would be seen on the movie screen. Twister and Willie stood just to the left of the director.

"Clear the set, we're ready to shoot."

The two women scurried from the ring like rabbits, and Mary and Jody had to cover their mouths to keep from laughing out loud.

"Quiet, please," shouted Mr. Gordon's assistant director. "Rolling."

A man appeared with a clapboard and held it in front of the camera. "Scene five, take one," he declared, snapping the hinged top of the board against the bottom, making a resounding clapping noise.

"Now I see why they call it a clapboard," Mary whispered.

"Speed," said another of the assistants, this one wearing headphones.

"And...action!" Mr. Gordon called.

Miss Beaumont turned her attention to the group of riders. "Now try and remember what I've just shown you," she instructed with a smile, "and let's mount up."

The riders in unison turned to their horses and, each placing their left foot in the stirrup, swung themselves up, landing squarely in the center of each of their saddles.

"Cut!" shouted Mr. Gordon.

Mary and Jody looked up in surprise and confusion. They thought everyone had done just as Mr. Gordon asked. But Mr. Gordon was gesturing toward the ring and saying something to Twister and Willie. A moment later, Twister walked over and leaned his arms on the top rail of the ring.

"Now, let's do that again, and this time some of you need to look like you're havin' a little trouble. Remember, this is the first time you've done this. So, let's see, let's have you, Mary...and you, Jeff, have trouble gettin' your foot in the stirrup. And a couple of you others, just fumble around a little bit gettin' up. Maybe you could have trouble throwin' your leg over the first time. Use your imagination."

"Hmph," Mary snorted, again addressing Jody from one side of her mouth. "Of all things, I would never have trouble getting my foot in the stirrup!"

"Mare, remember, it's a movie," Jody answered. Then she saw something from the corner of her eye. "Hey, look! There's my dad and your mom! They're watching from behind Mr. Gordon's chair!"

"Oh, my gosh! It is them!" Mare replied, grinning. "Now we really have to behave ourselves."

But there was no time for further conversation. Mr. Gordon was ready for take two.

"Quiet, please!"

"Rolling."

"Scene five, take two." Clap!

"Speed."

"And...action!"

Again, Vicki Beaumont turned to the riders. "Now try and remember what I just showed you," she repeated, "and let's mount up."

This time, the riders attempted to follow Mr. Gordon's direction. Mary fumbled with her stirrup, letting her foot slip out two or three times before getting it right. Jeff actually put his right foot instead of his left into the stirrup the first time, then sheepishly switched it. Jody grabbed the saddle horn and tried to swing her leg over but had to grab Shalimar's mane with the other hand before she could accomplish her mount. The others mounted much more slowly and awkwardly than before. Finally, all riders were mounted.

"Cut!" shouted Mr. Gordon.

"What the heck!" Mary said, loudly enough that Willie shot her a warning look.

"That was much better! Great, in fact!" Mr.

Gordon called. "Now let's do it one more time, and this time we'll continue the shot with Miss Beaumont giving you further instruction."

Once again, the riders dismounted. When the camera was ready, once again, Miss Beaumont said her line. This time, the riders had just managed to get their feet in the stirrups when they were interrupted by the man with the long, fuzzy-topped pole.

"Plane!" he shouted.

"Cut!" shouted Mr. Gordon.

"What in the world is going on?" Mary said in bewilderment. Her question was soon answered by the sight and sound of a low-flying small plane, which had picked just that moment to pass over the farm. Everything stopped until the plane was well out of sight.

"OK, back to one. Let's do it again," called Mr. Gordon's assistant.

"Scene one, take four!" Clap.

Thankfully, this time all was well, and the scene was allowed to continue. Vicki Beaumont instructed the riders to turn their horses to the rail, and they actually almost made it to their destination before Mr. Gordon interrupted.

*When Mrs. Morrow gave her a sympathetic
look and a thumbs-up, Mary sat up taller
in the saddle, ready to be quiet.*

"Cut!"

"Oh, my gosh, this is crazy," Mary exclaimed. This time, Willie walked over to the rail and leaned over.

"Mary Morrow, you need to keep quiet," he hissed. "I told you there would be a lot of stoppin' and startin', didn't I? This is how it's done. Now, after while, things'll get a little smoother, but you have to be patient. Each little bit of the scene is goin' to take three or four takes. You just have to get used to it," he finished more kindly, noticing Mary's face had flushed a deep red.

Mary simply nodded and glanced over to where her mother sat next to Jody's father. When Mrs. Morrow gave her a sympathetic look and a thumbs-up, Mary sat up taller in the saddle, ready to be quiet, no matter how many "takes" it took.

"All right, one more time," Mr. Gordon yelled.

The morning wore on, and just as Willie said, each small part of the riding scene needed to be repeated at least three times before Mr. Gordon was satisfied. Since this was supposed to be a beginner lesson, the riders were asked to perform no more than a walk on the rail. Miss Beaumont gave them instruction on keeping their heels down and toes up, their hands low on the withers, eyes straight ahead, heads high, and backs straight. Just as Mary thought she would go crazy if she heard the word "cut" one more time, Mr. Gordon's assistant approached the ring.

"Lunch!" he yelled.

"Yay!" Mary shouted and then clapped her hand over her mouth, looking guiltily at Willie, who tried to look stern but only managed a shake of his head.

Production assistants scurried around, shutting the power down on equipment and rolling cords up. Riders were instructed to dismount. The sound man lowered his fuzzy pole and removed his headphones.

"I guess that's where they get the expression, 'lower the boom,'" Jody suggested.

"I don't know about that. All I know is, I'm starving!" Mary exclaimed, leading Hoppy toward the gate. "I'm so glad we're finished!"

"Who said anything 'bout bein' finished?" Willie said, meeting the riders at the gate.

"But, Willie, that's the end of the scene, isn't it?" Mary asked.

"That's the end of the scene, but now they have to

switch the camera around and get a different angle," Willie replied nonchalantly.

"Oh, no," Mary groaned. "You mean we have to do it all over again? After lunch?"

"'Fraid so," Willie grinned. "Movie-makin' ain't as glamorous as you thought, now is it?"

"No, it's work!" Jody said wearily. Then, suddenly remembering her own pony, she turned to check on Lady.

"Here, I'll take Hoppy and Shalimar down to the stable," Willie offered, taking the reins from the girls' hands. Twister did the same for Jeff, who immediately scampered away toward the lunch tent. "Twister can handle Lady and Gypsy too, and you two can run up to lunch. We'll take care of the horses."

"Willie, are you sure?" Mary asked, hoping Willie was sure. She was tired and hungry and wanted nothing more than to pile her plate with the yummy food from the lunch buffet. "Thanks ever so!"

"Willie, would you mind checking on Star, too?" Jody cut in. "Poor thing must feel so neglected!"

"I'll check his water and give him some more hay," Willie assured her. "Now go on."

Before Willie could change his mind, Mary and Jody gave the horses one last pat on the neck and flew off to sample the treats that awaited them on the buffet.

Annie's Story

AS THE GIRLS HASTILY made their way to the lunch table, a thought suddenly occurred to Jody. She grabbed Mary's arm in mid-stride and slowed her to a walk.

"Mare, don't you think we should go in the farmhouse and check on Annie first? She's probably still scared and wondering why no one's come to see her."

"Good idea!" Mary cried, suddenly looking forward to the opportunity to question Annie about every aspect of the morning's incident. Jody, immediately recognizing the glint in her best friend's eye, kept her hand steady on Mary's arm.

"We probably shouldn't bother her with a bunch of questions," Jody warned. "Willie wouldn't like it, and she probably doesn't want to talk about it."

"Oh, Jody, don't be such a party pooper," Mary retorted. "She probably *does* want to talk about it, anyway. *I* would want to talk about it, if it happened to me."

"I'm sure you would," Jody said under her breath, knowing that she wouldn't be able to stop Mary from doing something once she set her mind to it.

The sight that met the girls' eyes when they entered the farmhouse stopped them in their tracks. Expecting to find Annie lying on the comfortable "davenport," as Mrs. McMurray called the over-stuffed sofa in the parlor, they were surprised to see her standing instead in the center of the roomy kitchen. Next to her, tilting the eyepiece of the movie camera so Annie could look through it, was the main cameraman.

"See, by just changing the camera angle, you get a completely different perspective on the scene you're shooting," the cameraman explained as Annie peered silently through the lens.

"Annie!" Mary cried, causing both Annie and her instructor to almost jump out of their skins.

"What?" Annie replied, turning quickly with an annoyed look at Mary.

"Sorry, Annie," Jody said sheepishly, giving Mary's arm an extra-hard squeeze. "We didn't mean to scare you. We just came up to see how you're doing."

"I'm doing fine. Why?" Annie asked, as though the events of the morning had left her mind completely.

"Well," Mary sputtered, "we thought...we thought you might like to have some company and maybe also tell us exactly what happened with Stumpy."

"Oh," replied Annie. Then she turned to the cameraman. "Thank you for the demonstration," she said politely.

Annie turned without a word and walked to the parlor, seating herself on the well-worn sofa. Mary and Jody glanced at each other and then followed her silently, each choosing a chair on either side of the sofa. They waited expectantly for Annie to speak. But waiting for Annie to speak was kind of like waiting for Willie to speak, only worse. Finally Mary could stand it no longer and broke the silence.

"So, Annie," she said nonchalantly, "why do you suppose Stumpy took off like that, out of the blue?"

Annie thought for a moment more before speaking. "Out of the blue?" she finally said. "I wouldn't say it was out of the blue."

Mary and Jody sat wide-eyed, waiting for Annie to continue. When they realized that they were waiting in vain, Jody took over the questioning.

"But, Annie, it seemed to us like he just took off. Did something scare him?"

"Well, of course something scared him," Annie snorted. "He's a nice, quiet boy. He wouldn't just take off for no reason."

Again they waited, and this time Mary prompted Annie to continue.

"Well, what do you suppose it was?" she asked. "And why were you riding him in the first place? Weren't you supposed to be just holding him?"

At this, Annie took a deep breath and looked down at her shoes.

"I know I was just supposed to be holding him," she sighed. "But I got really bored just standing there holding him and watching you guys ride around the ring. And I couldn't see very well, so I thought if I just got up and sat on his back I could see over the rail better, and I wouldn't be so bored. He didn't mind at all, and in fact he was just about falling asleep, when all of a sudden I heard this weird noise from the other side of the tree, and I saw something fly up in the air. I think it woke Stumpy up and scared him so bad at the same time that he just took off."

Mary and Jody sat motionless, mouths open, stunned at what was undoubtedly the longest speech they had ever heard from Annie. Mary finally recovered long enough to ask one more question.

"What do you think it was, Annie?"

Annie thought once more before replying.

"I think it was a ghost," she said matter-of-factly. "Now, I'm hungry. Can we go eat?"

As this conversation was taking place inside the farmhouse, another was playing out inside the Mooney house trailer. After settling the horses in their stalls, Willie had headed directly to the trailer, pulling on his earlobe and scratching the side of his head all the way there. Now he sat at the little kitchen table across from Jimmy, while Heath played with blocks on the living room floor. The only sound was the ticking of the old grandfather clock, one of the keepsakes that Mr. Mooney had managed to bring with him from his own farm after his wife died. Jimmy stared silently at the tabletop, his farm cap in his hands.

Willie took his own cap off and then spoke in his gentlest tone.

"Why don't you just tell me what happened, son?"

Jimmy just stared, then began to shake his head slowly from side to side until a solitary tear dripped from the end of his nose onto the tabletop.

"I didn't mean to do it," he said, his voice shaking. "I was just tryin' to figure out how that thing worked, and all of a sudden it just popped open and went flyin' up in the air and off to the side of the tree, and when that fool horse saw it he just took off a'runnin'. I didn't mean to do it!"

"I know you didn't, son. I saw you near the ring earlier on, lookin' at that reflector and studyin' it. After the horse took off, I looked around the tree to try to figure out what happened, and I saw it lyin' there in the grass, and I put two and two together. Now the good thing is that your sister didn't get hurt, just scared some. And if I know her, she'll forget about it in no time. I think the best thing is to 'fess up and just apologize and move on."

*Jimmy just stared, then began to shake his head
slowly from side to side until a solitary tear dripped
from the end of his nose onto the tablecloth.*

"What in heck is that thing supposed to be, anyway?" Jimmy cried, looking up for the first time.

"It's used in the movies to reflect light. It's made of a kind of nylon material, and it folds up into itself so you can store it in a small space. When you want to use it, you just give it a twist and it unfolds real quick. If you're not ready for it, it'll jump right out of your hands."

"It did that, all right. Scared the dickens out of me, worse than the horse."

Willie put his hand over Jimmy's for an instant and chuckled. "Could've happened to anybody. Nobody's gonna blame you for it, and if they do, they'll answer to me. Now why don't you gather up Heath there and we'll go up and find Annie and get us some lunch."

"Am I allowed? I'm not workin' on the movie or anything."

"You and Heath will be my guests. Lord knows they have enough food up there to feed the Confederate army."

After Annie's conversation with Mary and Jody had abruptly ended with the mention of a ghost, the three had made their way to the lunch buffet. Annie had just filled her plate in line at the buffet table when Jimmy, Heath, and Willie reached her. Mary and Jody were seated at a nearby table with heaping plates in front of them, eating as though they had been starving for days. But when the girls saw Jimmy put his arm around Annie and lead her away from the table, they dropped their forks.

"What's Jimmy doing up here?" Mary wondered, rising from her seat. "And what's he saying to Annie? Maybe I should go over there and see what's happening."

Jody once again grabbed Mary by the arm. "Mare, it's none of our business. You'd better just leave them alone. You know that's what Willie would say."

"Yes, that *is* what Willie would say," said Willie, leaning over between the two girls. "Now you better get to eatin' right quick, because we start again in five minutes. And no stickin' your noses in other people's business."

Mary blushed, and Jody groaned, but they finished their plates in five minutes flat and soon were back on the horses, endlessly going through their paces in the ring, following Vicki Beaumont's instructions over and over again. Just as the girls thought they would burst if they heard the words "rolling" or "cut" one more time, they heard a phrase they had not heard before.

"Checking the gate!" Mr. Gordon yelled.

Mary turned all the way around in her saddle so she could face Jody, who was behind her on Shalimar. "What does that mean?" she whispered loudly. "Why are they checking the gate? The gate's closed, just like it has been all day."

Willie, who was standing near the rail, overheard Mary's remark and actually laughed out loud. He held up his hand to signal Mary to come to a halt, then leaned over and smiled.

"Checking the gate means they're done shooting, Mary. There's a part of the camera called the gate. If everything's fine with it, they don't have to reshoot, and they're done for the day."

"Hallelujah!" Mary yelped and then clapped her hand over her mouth when several people turned to stare at her. Mr. Gordon just laughed.

"That's a wrap!" he shouted, and then looked directly at Mary. "Are you happy, young lady?"

"If a wrap means we're done, yes, sir," Mary blurted. Upon hearing the good news, Jenna Day and Krystal Warren jumped from their saddles and fairly threw their reins into the waiting hands of

Willie and Twister, who barely had time to enter the ring. Mary and Jody and Jeff Hunt were off their horses almost as quickly.

"Now hang on just a second," Twister called out. "Before you sign out, we want to thank you for your good work today. We know it was a long day, but you all did a great job. If you want to stay, you can get your dinner, and then you're all invited to a little campfire we're havin' down by the barn this evening to thank you for a job well done. Your parents are welcome, too."

Jenna Day and Krystal Warren looked at Twister and then at each other and took off at a trot through the gate, followed closely by Jeff Hunt. Mary and Jody were left holding Hoppy and Shalimar, while Twister and Willie gathered up the reins of Augie, Lady, and Gypsy. Without another word, the four led the horses down to Lucky Foot Stable, ready to settle them in for the night.

★ 15 ★
Willie's Past Revealed

A FESTIVE AIR PREVAILED over the bonfire that night, with everyone enjoying the opportunity to relax after a long day of filming. Twister and Willie had spent the early evening getting ready. The biggest logs in the woodpile were dragged with chains behind the old tractor and put into place in a circle. Rocks were gathered from around the barn and placed in a smaller inner circle to contain the fire. Short sticks were collected for kindling and longer ones for hot dog and marshmallow roasting. Just at twilight, Twister lit the fire, and people from the movie set began to gather.

The ever-present buffet table was nearby, but members of the film crew decided it was more fun roasting their own hot dogs over the fire. They milled about, talking and joking, happy to have a chance to relax. Finnegan, of course, insisted on making a nuisance of himself begging for samples, no matter how many times Twister shooed him away. Mary's mother and Jody's father sat on a log together, talking quietly while roasting marshmallows over the blaze.

Mary and Jody were the last to arrive, having finally finished their chores at Lucky Foot Stable. With so many horses in the barn, there was much more feeding and mucking to do than usual. The girls greeted their parents and then stood arm-in-arm next to Twister outside the circle of logs. While Jody gazed at the fire, Mary surveyed the crowd with curiosity.

"Twister, where are all the actors?" Mary whispered.

"Oh, the main actors usually don't show up for little parties like this," Twister explained. "And I think the kids that were in the scene with you are probably home sleepin' by now, not bein' used to such a long day. But you can be sure when you throw a little get-together, the crew'll show up, and sometimes the director."

Mary looked away, trying to hide her disappointment. She had hoped to see Brian McVey and maybe even carry on an intelligent conversation with him, so he could see she wasn't the ditzy girl she appeared to be.

"What about Willie?" Jody wondered. "Is he coming later?"

Twister gazed into the fire for a moment before answering. "I don't think Willie is going to make it tonight, Jody," he said somberly. "He's still pretty shook up from what happened to Annie today. I think it kind of reminded him of somethin'."

"Really?" Mary said, surprised. "I didn't think Willie seemed too upset this afternoon. He usually doesn't let things bother him for long. And what did it remind him of?"

Twister didn't reply but continued staring into the fire. After a long moment, he turned to the girls. "Why don't you two grab a couple of sticks and get yourselves some hot dogs or marshmallows or somethin'. Then come sit by me at the fire. I have somethin' to tell you."

Mary and Jody looked puzzled but did as Twister

said. Soon, they were settled on a log, long sticks in hand, turning their hot dogs over the fire. Finnegan sat nearby wagging his tail, greedily eyeing the roasting dogs.

"Finney, you can't possibly be hungry!" Mary laughed. "Everyone here has given you at least one hot dog already!"

"That dog won't know what to do with himself when the movie's finished," Twister said. "He's sure gonna miss all the attention."

Mary and Jody nodded silently, waiting in anticipation of whatever Twister was about to tell them. But Twister didn't seem in any hurry to speak, concentrating all of his attention on slowly turning his stick so that his marshmallow roasted perfectly on all sides. The girls had learned from experience with Willie that it probably wouldn't do any good to try to rush Twister. So they sat in silence. When their hot dogs were finally cooked, they went to the buffet table to get buns. By the time they came back to sit by Twister, he had carefully removed the marshmallow from the stick and was juggling it from one hand to the other to help it cool. It wasn't until the girls were halfway through their hot dogs that he finally cleared his throat.

*Soon, they were settled on a log, long sticks
in hand, turning their hot dogs over the fire.
Finnegan sat nearby wagging his tail.*

"I just want you to understand somethin'," Twister said quietly. "You don't need to repeat this to nobody, and you don't need to say anything to Will about it either."

Mary and Jody simply nodded, beginning to realize that what Twister was about to say was serious and that no reply was necessary.

Twister cleared his throat again before he continued. "You know that I worked with Will years ago on a movie set, somethin' like this one here. We knew each other even before that, when we rode in the army together, cavalry division."

At this, Mary couldn't hold her tongue. "Twister!" she exclaimed. "We were in Willie's house one day when we couldn't find Star, and we saw a picture of him in a uniform riding a horse. That was the cavalry picture, right?"

Twister chuckled. "Must be. I have that same picture myself. I'm the one sitting on my horse right next to Will."

The girls simply smiled and nodded, waiting for Twister to go on with his story. "Anyway, after the war, we went our separate ways, but just by chance ended up workin' in the wrangler business. I worked mostly on the East Coast, but Will was out west. So we never really worked together until one big picture came up. An epic, they called it."

"An epic!" Mary blurted. "Twister, I bet you didn't know that Jody and I are epic friends! That means, 'in the grand style, lofty in conception, and memorable!' I looked it up in the dictionary!"

Twister smiled. "That's what this picture was, all right. They needed lots of horses and lots of wranglers, so they called me to go out west and work on it. That's when Will and I caught up with each other."

Mary suddenly shivered and linked her arm through Jody's.

"Well, when I got out to the set Will was right happy to see me and took me around, helpin' me get acquainted with everybody. He was 'specially proud and happy to introduce me to his pretty new wife."

"His wife?" This time it was Jody who blurted out the question, while Mary simply opened her mouth in shock. "We...we never even knew Willie *had* a wife!"

"Oh, he had a wife all right. Shereen was her name, pretty as a picture, laughin' all the time. She was a wrangler, just like him. Willie used to puff up all proud and say that she was the only one he knew who could outride and out-rope him. And she proved it, too, workin' right there on the movie set, side by side with us."

Mary and Jody sat speechlessly staring at their half-eaten hot dogs. Twister paused and cleared his throat once again before going on with his story.

"Well, one day we were doin' stunt work on a real tough scene, where we had to round up some cattle into a pen. Shereen was dressed like a man, with her hair all tucked up under her hat so you couldn't tell she was a woman on camera. She was right in there with me and Will, like always, and we were just about done herdin' these cattle through the gate when one of 'em, a big longhorn bull, turned on us."

This time it was Jody who shivered, tempted to cover her ears so she wouldn't have to hear the rest of the story.

"That big longhorn whipped his head around, and the tip of his horn just barely caught the shoulder of Shereen's horse. He was a big, quiet quarter horse, but the sudden shock and pain made him rear straight up, and she came off."

"Oh, Twister, was she all right? I've fallen off plenty of times, and I was all right," Mary said hopefully, her voice shaking.

"Well, just fallin' off, maybe she would've been all right, but her boot got stuck in the stirrup, and the horse took off with her..."

"Oh, Twister, stop. I don't want to hear any more," Jody cried, this time covering her ears for real.

"I'm sorry, Jody. I won't go into it except to say that Will took off after that horse, just about like he did today. He leaned over and grabbed the reins and ended up slowin' it down enough so he could jump off his own horse. Her horse dragged him some and flipped him over, but he wouldn't let go until he got it stopped. He hurt his hip real bad, and that's why he has a limp to this day."

"And his wife...?" Mary whispered breathlessly.

"Will tried his best to save her, and the set doctor did all he could, but it was too late."

When Twister finished speaking, it seemed that the whole world had gone quiet. Mary and Jody stared silently into the fire, tears rolling down their cheeks.

"There's one more thing, and I won't say any more," Twister said so low that the girls had to lean over to hear his next words. "Will told me later that they had just found out Shereen was going to have a baby, so he didn't just lose his wife that day."

Mary and Jody drew in their breath at the same instant and gave in completely to the tears that flowed from the depths of their heartache for Willie. They wanted somehow at that instant to comfort him for the tragedy that happened so long ago, but they felt helpless.

"I didn't know if I should tell you, but I thought you should know," Twister said quietly. "Will thinks the world of you girls, and I think somehow you've been able to fill up some of the emptiness in his heart."

"Thank you for telling us, Twister," Jody said, her voice breaking.

"And we won't say anything to Willie." Mary added, wiping the tears from her cheeks with the back of her hand. "We'll just go on being his friends."

Caesar Arrives

MARY AND JODY arrived at Lucky Foot Stable the next morning just in time to see the big black truck pulling the silver horse trailer down the farm lane toward the road. Behind the wheel sat Willie, with Twister riding along in the passenger seat. Braking their bikes so abruptly that gravel went flying in all directions, the girls waved their arms, flagging Willie down before he could drive past. Willie slowed the truck until it came to a grinding halt just before the end of the lane.

"Willie!" Mary yelled, walking her bike up to the

window and peering in. "Where are you going?"

Willie tugged on his earlobe and glanced over at Twister. "Well, now, who wants to know?"

Mary and Jody looked at each other quizzically, then turned back to Willie. "We do," they said in unison.

"Hmph," Willie snorted, "you do, do you?"

"Willie! What's going on?" Mary said indignantly. Then a thought dawned on her, and she jumped up and down trying to see into the back of the trailer. "Willie! You're not taking the horses back to the auction, are you?"

"Well, I reckon I'm not, since this is Friday, not Monday, and the auction ain't even going on today," Willie replied calmly. "We're not goin' to drop somethin' off. We're goin' to pick somethin' up."

"Oh, Willie, what?" Jody squealed. "More horses?"

"Now, look, we wanted to get on our way before you girls got here and started buggin' us to death. You'll just have to wait 'til we come back to see what's goin' on. In the meantime, take care of the horses and git the stalls cleaned. By the time we come back, you'll be done, and you can see what we've got."

"But, but, Willie…" Mary began, but Willie revved the engine so that she was drowned out by the sound, and they drove off in a cloud of dust.

Mary and Jody watched silently as the truck drove down the road and disappeared from view and then turned their bikes toward Lucky Foot Stable. It wasn't until they were inside the coolness of the little stable that Mary found her voice. "I wonder what they're up to," she muttered to herself, then walked over and scratched Star between the ears. "I wonder what they're up to, Star," she repeated, as Star rubbed his head up and down on her forearm.

"Mare, let's try not to think about it," Jody said matter-of-factly. "We've got work to do. Why don't you put hay out in the paddock for Augie and Hoppy, and I'll put Star, Shalimar, and Stumpy on crossties in the aisle so we can clean the stalls. Then we've got to bring Augie and Hoppy in and turn Shalimar and Stumpy out. And we've got to visit Lady and Gypsy in the big pasture. And we'll have to take Star out for a walk, since he's stuck in his stall so much right now."

With so many horses and only three stalls in Lucky Foot Stable, it was a juggling act to make sure that everyone had a chance to be turned out in the paddock for at least part of the day or night. The girls kept busy for the next two hours, leading horses in and out, cleaning stalls, grooming Star, filling water buckets, and sweeping the aisle. Finally it was time to take the frisky colt out for his walk.

"Why don't we lead him out to the big pasture so we can visit Lady and Gypsy?" Jody suggested. "Then we can kill two birds with one stone, as Willie would say."

"Good plan," Mary agreed. She snapped the lead rope onto Star's halter and led him from his stall. "And, since we've already groomed him, let's put his saddle and bridle on. It never hurts to keep up with his training!"

But even before the girls had the chance to get Star's saddle from the tack trunk, the low growl of the truck engine could be heard in the distance. Star pricked up his ears at the sound, and Finnegan awakened from his morning nap. Jody flew to the back of the stable and looked out the back doors.

"Mare! It's Willie and Twister, back already! Oh, Star, you'll have to wait just a little longer for your walk!"

Mary turned and hastily led Star back into his stall, where he snorted and pawed impatiently as if to say, "Hey! I want to see what's going on too!"

"Star, I promise, we'll be back as soon as we see what Willie and Twister are up to!"

With that, the girls ran out to the gravel lane just in time for the big truck to pass by the stable on its way to the farmhouse. Twister grinned impishly and waved at the girls, ignoring their attempts to wave the truck to a stop. When they saw that Willie was really not going to stop at Lucky Foot, they took off at a gallop after the truck and trailer, Finnegan nipping at their heels. By the time Willie braked to a stop just outside the farmhouse, the girls were red-faced and completely out of breath. But that didn't stop them from jumping up and down in an attempt to see what was inside the trailer.

"Willie!" Mary called the instant Willie stepped from the truck cab. "Where did you go, and what did you get?"

"Now, just hold yer horses," Willie said, grinning in spite of himself, "and stand back while me and Twister unload. Matter of fact, why don't you just cover yer eyes 'til I tell you to look."

It was all Mary and Jody could do to stand back and cover their eyes, but they did as Willie said. Even Finnegan sat silently, wagging his tail in anticipation. The next sound was the creaking of the trailer door opening, followed by a metallic clank of ramps put in place, then a crunching of wheels turning on gravel. Last, a more familiar sound—hooves stepping from the trailer and walking in a circle.

Still, Willie said nothing to the girls. At last, they could stand it no longer.

"Willie!" Jody cried. "Can we look now?"

"Oh, I almost forgot," Willie chuckled. "Yes, you can look."

Mary and Jody dropped their hands from their eyes and blinked once. Then, the vision that greeted them made their eyes and mouths fly open wide and made Twister laugh at the sight of the two astonished girls.

Resting on the gravel lane, in all its magnificence, stood a dazzling white Cinderella carriage, complete with elegantly curved patent leather fenders and royal blue velvet seats. A pair of brass carriage lamps glistened in the sun on either side of the driver's seat. A delicate, rounded step descended from an arched support to allow easy access to the two seats of the carriage, where passengers could sit facing each other. And the crowned top of the carriage was folded down and back for an open ride in the warm afternoon breeze.

But even more thrilling for Mary and Jody was the sight of the carriage horse, standing as still as a statue in Twister's grasp as if waiting patiently to be hitched up. He was very light gray, almost white, with a sprinkling of shiny dapples over his loin. The crest of his neck formed a perfect arch as he bent his head to sniff a spot on Twister's shoulder. He was the tallest and broadest horse the girls had ever seen, but his eyes were so kind that they felt no fear of him.

"Ooh," Jody sighed, exhaling for the first time since she caught sight of the carriage and horse.

"Oh, Willie," Mary whispered, reaching out to touch the smooth leather surface of the dashboard. "Where in the world did you get this? What are we going to do with it? Is it for the movie? Do we get to keep it? What's the horse's name? He's so beautiful!"

"Now, which question do you want me to answer first?" Willie asked, grinning at the look of awe on the faces of the girls. "Fact is, I rented it from a carriage company in the city. We're gonna use it for the last scene of the movie. No, we don't get to keep the carriage or the horse, either one. And his name is Caesar."

"We don't get to keep it, but it'll be here all day today, and maybe tomorrow, depending on how

But even more thrilling for Mary and Jody
was the sight of the carriage horse, standing
as still as a statue in Twister's grasp.

filming goes," Twister added. "We're gonna be hitchin' up soon, and as soon as Will's ready and the camera's set up, we'll get started."

"Oh, Twister, can we watch?" Jody pleaded, "We won't get in the way or make noise or anything, we promise."

"Now, it's gonna be a while, and besides, don't you have more work to do?" Willie replied before Twister had the chance. "I know you didn't get everything done in the stable already."

"Well...we almost did. We just have to take Star for a walk and visit Lady and Gypsy in the big pasture and check the water and hay in the paddock," Mary said breathlessly.

"Then git on down there and finish up, and by that time, maybe we'll be ready to shoot," Willie said. "And don't go rushin' around like crazy. You ain't gonna miss anything."

Before Willie had even finished his sentence, the girls were halfway to the stable. Upon their arrival, Star nickered and pawed impatiently in his stall.

"Sorry, buddy," Jody said, hastily opening the stall and clipping a lead rope on Star's halter. "We came back as fast as we could!"

Just as planned, Star was led to the big pasture, where Lady and Gypsy stood muzzle to muzzle under the weeping willow tree, switching their tails at flies. The cows raised their heads curiously as the girls trotted past with Star in tow but soon lost interest and lowered their heads to graze. The ponies greeted Star by sniffing noses in turn, and then Mary and Jody told them all about the dazzling carriage and Caesar, the gorgeous carriage horse.

"Of course, you are far more beautiful," Mary assured them for fear of hurting their feelings, although they didn't look offended in the least.

"Mare, I think we should go back now and switch the horses out of the paddock so Star can go out," Jody said anxiously. "They're probably ready to start filming by now. And we still have to check hay and water!"

"Good plan. Let's go!" Mary shouted, and just as quickly as they had entered the pasture, they were out again and finishing up final chores at Lucky Foot.

★ 17 ★
Happy Endings

ALTHOUGH ONLY AN hour had passed since the girls had left the farmhouse, they were surprised to see how much progress had been made when they returned. Crew members were milling about, putting final touches on the lighting and sound. Two cameras were set up, and Mr. Gordon was already studying the monitor. Mary was thrilled to see Brian McVey standing near the door of the farmhouse, looking very handsome in a black tuxedo! Caesar, resplendent in a shiny black harness, was hitched to the carriage, with Twister standing at his head.

Trying not to attract attention, Mary and Jody nonchalantly sauntered up to Twister and began asking questions.

"Twister!" Mary whispered loudly. "What's happening?"

"Why is Caesar hooked to the carriage?" Jody continued.

"This is the last scene of the movie, where Brian and Vicki's characters get married in the farmhouse." Twister replied. "When they come out, they'll get in the carriage and drive away."

"Are they getting ready to get married right now? In the farmhouse?"

Twister chuckled. "No, no, they already shot that scene a few days ago. All we're shooting now is them coming out, like as if they just got married, and they get in the carriage. Then they kiss, and the carriage takes them away."

Mary and Jody giggled at the thought of Brian McVey actually kissing Vicki Beaumont. Then Twister gave them a sly smile.

"Hmm, here comes the carriage driver now," he said, drawing out his words as he pointed toward the farmhouse.

"Wow, he's dressed up almost as fancy as the

groom," Jody observed, taking in the driver's black suit, bow tie, and shiny black top hat in one glance.

"Yeah, he sure looks..." Mary began, and then she stopped. Her eyes widened, and her mouth dropped open, shut tight, and then opened again. She pointed wordlessly, then found her voice. "Jody, Jody... That's...That's..."

Jody looked at Mary and then back at the carriage driver. Then it was her turn to gasp in shock. "Willie!" she shrieked.

And it was Willie. But the girls had never seen Willie quite like this before. His silver hair, peeking out from beneath the top hat, was slicked back on either side. Covering his gnarly hands was an elegant pair of black driving gloves. His feet were shod in shiny black shoes. And the woman who was normally fussing with Vicki Beaumont's hair was now bustling around Willie, comb in hand, making sure not one silver strand of hair was out of place!

Twister laughed out loud at the girls' expressions. "What's a'matter? You never seen Will dressed up before?"

Mary gulped before replying. "Twister! We've never seen Willie in anything except his barn clothes! Why, he's...he's...he's..."

"Handsome!" Jody exclaimed in disbelief.

"Yes. He's handsome," Mary agreed matter-of-factly. "Twister, how did he get the job driving the carriage? Don't they have to hire a real actor for that?"

"He got the job because he's the head wrangler, and he knows how to drive a carriage, and he's just the best man for the job. He doesn't have any lines to say, he's just goin' to sit up there and drive the horse, that's all. And look handsome, o'course," Twister finished, rolling his eyes.

"Twister, can we go talk to him?" Jody asked, feeling shy all of a sudden.

"Well, I reckon so. They haven't started shooting yet." Twister looked down at the two girls. "What are you two lookin' all blushy about? It's just Will, dressed up in a penguin suit."

Twister's description of Willie's ensemble made the girls giggle, and, forgetting their shyness, they walked over to the door of the farmhouse arm in arm. Willie's back was turned to them as the hairdresser smoothed down a few stray hairs for the hundredth time.

"Ahem, excuse us, sir, but..."

Willie turned to face the girls.

"Could we have your autograph?"

"Oh, quit your foolishness," Willie harrumphed, pulling at the collar of the starched white shirt. But the girls could see he was secretly pleased, even turning a little red himself.

"Willie, we hardly recognized you!" Jody chirped. "You look so...so..."

"Handsome!" Mary shouted.

"Shush now, girl," Willie said, blushing more deeply as he looked around at the bustling movie set. "The sooner we get this over with and I can get this doggoned straitjacket off, the gladder I'll be."

"Well, Willie, my goodness, don't you look..."

"Mom! What are you doing here?" Mary spun around at the sound of her mother's voice.

"And Dad!" Jody exclaimed. Mr. Stafford reached out to shake Willie's hand and then turned smiling to Jody. "Well, now, do you two think you're the only ones allowed to hang around the set? Willie invited us down to take a look at the carriage."

"Oh, Daddy, isn't it beautiful?" Jody breathed. "Wouldn't it be heavenly to take a ride in it?"

"It sure would." Mary's mom and Jody's dad exchanged glances.

"And Mom," Mary said excitedly, taking her

mother's hand, "come pet Caesar. He's really big, but he's about as gentle as a lamb."

Mary's mom allowed herself to be led to Caesar's huge head. When she tentatively put out her hand and stroked his muzzle, Caesar closed his eyes and sighed.

"See, Mom? He likes you! Now, Twister said they're just about to film this scene where Brian and Vicki get married and ride away in the carriage. Can you stay and watch? Please?"

"Well, I guess so, if Frank says it's all right. We drove over here together. I think he is planning on staying a while."

"Oh, goody! I think it's OK if we stand right over here."

"Quiet! Quiet, please! We're ready to roll! Last looks!" Mr. Gordon boomed through his megaphone. The hairdresser smoothed Willie's hair one more time, and the wardrobe lady straightened his tie. Twister stood at Caesar's head while Willie climbed onto the driver's seat of the carriage and gathered up the reins. Sitting straight as an arrow, dignified in his top hat and suit, Willie almost looked young again. Mary and Jody, standing with their parents on either side, gazed at Willie in awe and then looked at each other, grinning through teary eyes and not feeling the least bit embarrassed about it.

"Quiet, please!" It was the assistant director yelling this time. Then, "Rolling! And...action!"

The door of the farmhouse burst open. Brian emerged first, pulling a laughing Vicki by the hand through the open doorway. A crowd of well-wishers followed, throwing rice and shouting their congratulations. The wedding photographer and most of the guests snapped away as the smiling couple ran to the carriage and climbed in.

"Look at Caesar," Mary whispered to Jody. "He's being such a good boy! He hasn't budged at all, even with all the commotion!"

"Cut!" yelled Mr. Gordon, just as Willie gave Caesar the command to move forward by tapping him on the rump with the carriage whip.

"That was great. Let's do it again. Back to one!"

"If it was so great, why do they have to do it again?" Jody's father asked. "And what's he mean, 'back to one'?"

"Dad, they do everything way more than once. You just have to get used to it," Jody explained.

"That means everybody goes back to the places

they were at first so they can start all over," Mary explained.

"Yeah, Daddy, don't you remember the day you watched us in the ring? We did everything at least twice," Jody said.

"Yes, Frank, don't you know anything about moviemaking?" Mary's mom asked with a smile.

"Oh, excuse me, Katherine. I'll wait for you to explain everything to me from now on."

Mary and Jody's parents locked eyes and smiled for so long that Mary nudged Jody, and Jody looked at Mary quizzically. Finally they shrugged in unison and turned their attention back to business. Willie had turned Caesar in a circle so that he was standing in the exact same spot, and it was time to shoot.

"And...action!" The door burst open again, rice came flying, Brian and Vicki climbed in the carriage, and this time Caesar actually trotted a few steps before Mr. Gordon called, "Cut!" Then, "Reloading!"

"What's happening now?" Mary's mom whispered.

"Oh, the camera needs to have its film reloaded," Jody explained patiently. "It just takes a few minutes."

Just then, Mary caught a sudden movement out of the corner of her eye, over near the old horse chestnut tree. When she turned her head, she saw Annie Mooney peeking out from behind the tree, watching the filming. In that instant, Annie saw Mary watching her, and she turned and tiptoed away.

"Annie! Wait!" Mary yelled, grabbing Jody by the hand. Running together, they soon caught up with Annie, who was on her way back to the house trailer. "What's wrong, Annie?" Mary asked breathlessly. "Why don't you come watch with us?"

"Me?" Annie said, looking at the ground as she walked. "Oh, well, I never really got to be in the movie or anything."

"So?" Jody said.

"So I didn't know if I was allowed so close up."

Mary snorted. "Well, of course you're allowed, Annie. You were already on the set the day they filmed the riding scene, and..."

"I know," Annie interrupted. "That's why. I didn't think they would want me around after that."

"Annie, what are you talking about? That wasn't even your fault," Jody said.

"But it was!" Annie exclaimed, spinning around suddenly to face the girls. "I wasn't supposed to be sitting on Stumpy, and then he took off, and I couldn't hold on, and Willie had to rescue me, and at first it didn't seem so bad, but then I thought and thought about it, and I knew they would never give me another chance to be in the movie, and it was just the worst thing that's ever happened to me in my whole life!"

Mary and Jody were rendered speechless by this, one of the longest sentences Annie had ever uttered. But when they saw tears springing to her eyes, they quickly recovered their voices.

"Aw, Annie, don't worry about it," Mary said gently. "Nobody blamed you for it. It could've happened to anybody. Now, come on, why don't you come back with us and watch?"

"Yeah, Annie, you haven't even seen Caesar up close," Jody continued. "I bet he'll just love you."

Annie stopped, squared her shoulders, and wiped her nose with the back of her hand. Then she nodded without a word and turned back toward the movie set. Mary and Jody smiled at each other, trailing a step behind.

The three girls walked quietly for a minute, but as they neared the set Mary thought of a topic to break the silence. "Our parents came to watch today, too, Annie. They're really acting goofy."

"Yeah," added Jody. "They were looking all googly-eyed at each other."

"Well, they're in love, you know," Annie said.

Mary and Jody stopped in their tracks. They looked at each other again, but this time they weren't smiling.

"What did you say, Annie?" gulped Mary.

"I said they're in love," Annie repeated.

"But, but...what do you mean?" Jody sputtered.

"What do you mean, what do I mean?" Annie stopped walking to face the girls. "Didn't you know? I mean, anybody can see it. Can't you?"

The girls gulped and stood staring at each other. Then they turned in unison and looked at their parents, who were standing just out of camera range, grinning and whispering like teenagers.

"Checking the gate!" yelled Mr. Gordon.

"Come on, that means they're done filming!" Mary exclaimed, grabbing Jody by the hand. In the next instant, the girls were standing, hands on hips, in front of their surprised parents. Annie crept over to Caesar, who immediately began licking her hand.

"Hey, girls. Where did you go off to?" Jody's dad asked, a bemused look on his face.

"What in the world is the matter?" continued

Mary's mom, reacting to the girls' expressions.

"Dad, we have to ask you something," Jody said breathlessly.

"OK, shoot."

Mary and Jody stood silently, gazing anxiously from one parent to the other.

"Mary, what is it, for Pete's sake?" Mary's mother asked.

The girls gulped, and the question came bursting forth from both lips at the same instant.

"Are you in love?"

Mary's mother gasped and took a step back. Jody's father simply grinned and shook his head. Then he took Jody's hand in his.

"We were wondering when you two would figure us out," he said gently. "Jody, we were going to sit you and Mary down tonight and have a talk about it. We've had these feelings for some time, but we wanted to be absolutely sure before we brought you two into it. We didn't want you to be hurt if it turned out not to be real."

Mary stared at her mom. "And...and...is it real, Mom?"

Mrs. Morrow nodded slowly, tears coming to her eyes. "Oh, yes, Mary. It is definitely real."

They turned in unison and looked at their parents,
who were standing just out of camera range,
grinning and whispering like teenagers.

"It was funny what you said about taking a ride in the carriage, Jody," her father continued, "because that's one reason we're here today. Willie thought we should see it if we want to use it ourselves sometime in the future."

Mary and Jody stared silently while this idea slowly sank into their brains. "You mean...you would use the carriage for...for..." Mary began.

"And Willie...Willie knew about this all along?" Jody finished.

"Well, why don't you ask him yourself?"

Willie suddenly appeared behind the girls as if on cue, tie loosened and top hat removed. He stood scratching both sides of his head as if to get rid of the "goop" that had been applied to his hair. "Ask me what?" he said, looking down at the two girls.

"Willie!" Mary exclaimed, "why didn't you tell us why you really asked my mom and Jody's dad to the set today?"

Willie exchanged sheepish looks with the parents before answering. "Well, I guess it wasn't my place to tell you. But now I guess you've been told."

"Yes, but they didn't tell us," Jody said.

"Annie told us!" Mary practically shouted. "She figured it out!"

At the sound of her name, Annie smiled and gave a little wave. Caesar, thinking he was about to be ignored, shoved her with his giant nose, almost knocking her over. At that, the serious group broke into laughter, and the ice was broken.

Then Mary, always the first to think ahead, knitted her brow and appeared deep in thought. Suddenly, she looked up, as if a light bulb had gone off in her head. She grabbed both of Jody's hands in hers.

"Jody!" she screeched. "Do you know what this means? Do you get it? Do you get it?

It means that we, you and I, are going to be..."

The realization sunk in with Jody, and a brilliant smile lit up her face.

"SISTERS!" The girls shouted in unison.

Glossary of Horse Terms

Bale—In stable terms, a bale is a closely packed bundle of either hay or straw (see definitions) measuring about two by three feet, weighing about forty pounds, and tied with two strings lengthwise. When the strings are cut, the bale can be shaken loose and either fed, in the case of hay, or used for stall bedding, in the case of straw.

Baling twine—The term used for the thick yellow string that is tied around a bale.

Bank barn—A barn that is built into the side of a hill so the hill forms a "ramp" leading into the upper part of the barn, where hay and straw may be stored; the bottom floor of the barn is used for milking cows if it is a dairy barn, or it may have stalls for the purpose of sheltering other animals.

Barn swallow—A small, blue-black bird with a rusty-colored breast and throat and forked tail; found all over North America and Europe, these friendly birds like to build their nests in barns and eat insects.

Barrel—The middle section of the body of a horse or pony between the shoulder and the flank.

Bay—A common color seen in horses and ponies. The body is reddish-brown with black mane, tail, and lower legs.

Bit—The metal piece on the bridle inserted into the mouth of a horse that provides communication between the rider and horse.

Boom—A large, plush-covered microphone that picks up the dialogue and other sounds on a movie set. It is normally held on a pole by a sound person above the actors' heads.

Bosal—The braided rawhide or rope noseband of a hackamore-type bridle, knotted under the horse's jaw.

Bridle—The leather headgear with a metal bit that is placed on the head of a horse to enable the rider to control the horse.

Bridle path—A section of mane about an inch wide behind the ears that is trimmed short to allow the crown piece of the bridle to lie flat and fit more comfortably.

Call time—The time of day that an actor is required to be on the movie set.

Cannon bone—A bone in the leg of the horse or pony running from the knee, or hock, to the ankle.

Cantankerous—Ill-mannered or quarrelsome.

Canter—A three-beat gait of the horse, which could be called a "collected gallop." It is slightly faster and not as "bouncy" as a trot.

Chaff—The seed covering separated from the seed when grain is threshed.

Chestnut—A common coloring found in horses and ponies. The coat is basically red, in varying shades on different horses. The mane and tail are the same color as the body.

Cinch—The girth of the western saddle that fastens around the heart girth of the horse, holding the saddle in place.

Cluck—The "clicking" sound a rider or driver makes from the corner of the mouth to urge a horse forward. Also the sound a chicken makes when communicating.

Corncob—The inner segment of an ear of corn to which the corn kernels are attached. The horse eats the kernels but not the cob.

Crop—A short, leather riding whip carried by the rider and used lightly to encourage the horse to move forward.

Crosstie—The method of tying a horse squarely in the aisle or stall by which a rope is clipped to both sides of the halter. When a horse is crosstied, he cannot move away from the rider during grooming and saddling.

Dam—The mother of a horse or pony.

Dismount—The action of getting down from a horse and onto the ground.

Dock—The bone in a horse's tail, which is formed of the lowest vertebrae of the spine.

Draft horse—A type of horse characterized by a heavy build; typically used for field work and other types of pulling and driving. Breeds include Belgian and Clydesdale.

Dutch door—A door divided horizontally in the middle so the two sections can be opened separately.

Eaves—The overhanging lower edge of a roof.

Fetlock—The part of the lower leg of the horse or pony between the cannon bone and the pastern.

Flake—A section of hay that is taken from a bale for feeding, usually about six inches wide and two feet square. There are usually about ten flakes of hay in a whole bale.

Flaxen—A cream-colored mane and tail sometimes found on chestnut horses and always found on palominos. If a chestnut has a flaxen mane and tail, he is known as a "flaxen chestnut."

Foal—A young, unweaned horse or pony of either gender. When the horse or pony is weaned or separated from its mother, it is called a "weanling."

Forelock—The lock of hair falling forward over the face of the horse.

Founder—A painful disease of the foot that may be caused by the overeating of grass or grain when the digestive system of the horse or pony is not used to it. This may cause the tissues and blood vessels inside the hoof to be permanently damaged.

Gallop—A fast, four-beat gait where all four of the horse's feet strike the ground separately.

Garner—To acquire by effort.

Giving the horse his head—Allowing the horse or pony to stretch his neck and feel his way along rather than keeping a tight rein on him.

Grain—Harvested cereals or other edible seeds, including oats, corn, wheat, and barley. Horses and ponies often eat a mixture of grains, vitamins, minerals, and molasses called "sweet feed."

Gray—A common color found in horses and ponies. A gray horse is born black and gradually lightens with age from a steel-gray color to almost white.

Graze—The act of eating grass. Horses and ponies will graze continually when turned out on good pasture.

Groom—To groom a horse is to clean and brush his coat, comb his mane and tail, and pick the dirt from his hooves. A person known as a "groom" goes along on a horse show or horse race to help with grooming, tacking up, or anything else that needs to be done.

Hackamore—A bitless bridle used in the West for training horses.

Halter—Also known as a "head collar," a halter is made of rope, leather, or nylon and is placed on the head of a horse and used for leading or tying him. The halter has no bit, but it has a metal ring that rests under the chin of the horse or pony to which is attached a lead rope.

Hard brush—A grooming tool resembling a scrub brush, usually with firm bristles made of nylon, used to brush dried mud or dirt from the coat and legs of a horse or pony.

Haunches—Another term for the hindquarters of a horse or pony.

Hay—Grass or other herbage that is cut in the field and allowed to dry over several days, then usually baled and stored in a barn to be used as feed for animals.

Hay net—A nylon or rope net that is stuffed with loose hay and tied at the top, then hung in a stall or trailer to allow an animal to eat from it.

Heifer—A young cow that has not yet birthed a calf.

Hindquarters—The rear of a horse or pony, including the back legs.

Hitch up—Attach a horse or pony to a cart, carriage, or sleigh with the harness straps.

Hoof pick—A grooming tool used to clean dirt and gravel from the hooves of a horse or pony.

Hooves—The hard covering of the foot of a horse or pony. The hooves must be cleaned before and after riding and trimmed every six weeks (or so) to keep them from growing too long.

In hand—Refers to horses shown in halter classes, not mounted.

Interior—A movie scene that is shot inside a building rather than outside.

Last looks—A term used by a movie director to warn the hair and makeup crew that the shot is about to take place and they should exit camera range.

Lead rope—A short (about six feet) length of cotton or nylon rope with a snap attached to the end. The rope is used to lead the horse or pony.

Lead shank—Same as a lead rope, but it is more often made of leather, with a section near the snap made of chain.

Leather conditioner—An oily or creamy substance that is rubbed into leather to help keep it from drying out and cracking.

Leg up—The action of helping someone mount by grasping their bended left knee and hoisting them up and onto the back of the horse or pony.

Liniment—A liquid solution rubbed onto sore muscles to relieve pain.

Lipped—To touch or feel with the lips.

Loft—The large, open area in the top of a barn used to store bales of hay and straw.

Longe whip—A long whip used along with the longe line to encourage a horse or pony to move in a circle.

Mane—The long hair that grows on the crest (top) of a horse's or pony's neck.

Mane and tail comb—Any of a variety of metal or plastic combs used to comb the mane and tail of the horse or pony.

Mare—A female horse or pony three years of age or older.

Mare's tails—Also known as cirrus clouds, these are wispy cloud formations that actually look like the long, flowing tail of a horse or pony.

Milk house—The small building attached to a dairy barn where the milk ends up in a cooling tank.

Muzzle—The lower end of the nose of a horse or pony, which includes the nostrils, lips, and chin.

Neat's-foot oil—A type of oil used to condition leather to keep it from drying out and cracking.

Nicker—A low, quiet sound made by a horse or pony in greeting or when wanting to be fed.

Paddock—A fenced area, smaller than a field, used for enclosing animals for limited exercise.

Pastern—The lower part of the leg of a horse or pony below the fetlock and above the hoof.

Piebald—A horse or pony with a black coat color and white patches or markings on various parts of its body.

Pinto—A horse or pony with a solid coat color and white patches or markings on various parts of the body. The mane and tail may be various colors.

Pony—A pony measures below 14.3 hands from the bottom of the hoof to the withers. (See definition.) A hand equals four inches. An animal 14.3 hands or above is considered a horse.

Progeny—The offspring or descendants of one or both parents.

Pulling comb—A small, metal, short-toothed comb used to thin or shorten the hairs of the mane.

Quarter horse—A strong, stocky, but gentle breed of horse whose name is derived from its speed at the quarter-mile race. This breed is very popular with cow ropers and Western riders.

Quiet—Term used to describe a horse that is very gentle and easy to work with.

Rail—The term used in riding lessons and horse shows to describe the fencing enclosing the riding ring. To be "on the rail" is to be riding closely to the ring fence. Spectators standing outside the ring are said to be "at the rail."

Reins—The leather straps of the bridle attached to the bit and held by the rider to guide and control the horse.

Ringmaster—The person at a horse show who assists the judge in the ring and helps any rider who falls; this person may also replace any rails that are knocked down during jumps.

Saddle—A padded leather seat for a rider, placed on a horse's or pony's back and secured by a girth. A harness placed on the horse's or pony's back behind the withers is also called a saddle.

Saddlebags—Two leather pouches attached to each other by a wide piece of leather that drapes over the saddle or withers of the horse, or sometimes behind the saddle, to allow the rider to carry supplies on the trail.

Saddle rack—A metal or wooden frame attached to the wall or stall on which to hang the saddle.

Saddle soap—A creamy soap in a can used to soften and clean leather. The soap is rubbed into the leather and then buffed with a cloth.

Salt block—A square, compact brick made of salt placed in the field or stall for a horse to lick, which provides him with salt and other necessary minerals.

Scrubby mitt—A rubber mitt with short bristles on one side that fits over the hand and is used to bathe a horse or pony.

Singeing pan—A low-sided pan containing a small amount of burning lighter fluid that produces a small flame. When passed briefly over this flame, the hair-like under feathers of poultry are removed.

Sire—The father of a horse or pony.

Skewbald—A horse or pony with a coat color other than black combined with white patches or markings on various parts of the body.

Sleigh—A horse-drawn vehicle that does not have wheels but "runners" for gliding over snow or ice.

Slipknot—A type of knot, also known as "quick release," which can be quickly and easily untied in case of a problem, such as a horse or pony falling down or getting hung up.

Soft brush—A brush made for grooming a horse or pony's coat and face; it is the same shape as a hard brush, but has softer, longer bristles.

Sound—Term used to describe a horse that is free from injury, flaw, blemishes, and lameness.

Speed—A movie term meaning the sound recording device is "up to speed," or ready to record the sound.

Spook—An action of the horse or pony in which he shies away nervously from something he is not familiar with.

Springtooth harrow—A piece of farm machinery with curved teeth used to dig furrows into the ground for planting.

Square up—A horse or pony is said to be "standing square" or "squared up" when all four legs are placed evenly on the ground, the two front lined up so no one foot is in front of or behind the other, and hind feet are the same. This is the desirable position when showing the animal at halter.

Stallion—A male horse or pony that has not been neutered and may be used for reproductive purposes.

Star—Any white mark on the forehead of a horse or pony, located above the level of the eyes.

Straw—The material used as bedding in a stall; it consists of stalks of grain from which the grain has been removed and the stalks baled. It should be bright yellow and not dusty.

Sweat scraper—A tool made of plastic or metal that is held in the hand and used to remove excess sweat from a hot horse or pony or excess water from one being bathed.

Tack—Equipment used in riding and driving horses or ponies, such as saddles, bridles, harnesses, etc.

Tack box—A container with a handle used to transport grooming tools, bridles, etc., to horse shows or other events.

Tack trunk—A large trunk usually kept in the stable, which contains the equipment used by the rider, such as as bridles, grooming tools, saddles, lead ropes, medicines, etc.

Throatlatch—The narrow strap of the bridle, which goes under the horse's throat and is used to secure the bridle to the head.

Trot—A rapid, two-beat gait in which the front foot and the opposite hind foot take off at the same time and strike the ground simultaneously.

Trough—A long, shallow receptacle used for feeding or watering animals.

Wash stall—An enclosed area, usually inside the stable, with hot and cold running water, where a horse or pony may be crosstied and bathed.

Weanling—A foal who has been weaned (separated) from its mother and is no longer nursing. Foals are normally weaned at about six months of age.

Whinny—A high-pitched, loud call of the horse.

Winter coat—The longish hair that a horse or pony naturally grows in the winter to protect him from the cold. In the spring, the winter coat "sheds out" and the body becomes sleek again, with a short hair coat.

Withers—The ridge at the base of the neck and between the shoulders of a horse or pony. The saddle sits on the horse's back behind the withers, and the distance the horse or pony's height is measured by measuring from the ground to the top of the withers.

Wrangler—In movie terms, a wrangler is a person who provides horses and other animals to the movie set and/or cares for them and prepares them for their scenes.

Wrapped—A movie term meaning a certain scene and/or the entire movie is finished shooting.

JoAnn Dawson with Painted Warrior

About the Author

A horse lover since childhood, JoAnn Dawson lives with her husband, Ted, and their two sons on a horse farm in Maryland, where they operate a bed & breakfast and offer riding lessons, carriage rides, horse shows, and a summer camp. JoAnn teaches Equine Science at a local college and is an actress and animal wrangler for film and television. She has enjoyed competing over the years on her American Paint Horse, Painted Warrior, but it is Butterscotch the pony who accompanies her on school visits and book signings. Butterscotch is so comfortable around kids that he may be the only pony in the country who is allowed to go into classrooms! Learn more about the author and her farm at www.luckyfootseries.com.